Starcrossed Poetry

Anthology I

Poems by Author

Starcrossed

Watching humans write is intimate.
The way they tilt their heads down,
the shape of their mouths,
the way their eyes dart back and forth over the page,
the way they pause to consider their words.
Consternation as they discuss constellations,
the universe expanding,
and the separation of our very molecules
with the movement of pen on page.
And even as our galaxy pulls steadily apart,
we cling to each other.
Knowing that when we feel loneliest,
it is better to reach for the next nearest star
than to go out alone.
Calling each other in,
"My darling, let my warmth infect you,
bring you back to burning."

If separation is how we end?
Come together, come together, come together.

Andie Arlo

Chapter 1:

<u>Hollywood Forever</u>

I once told a man
that I loved him
and that I talked to ghosts.

He vanished.

I guess he got spooked
that I could see right through him.

-Andie Arlo

Chapter 2:

<u>Samson</u>

She took to him with scissors,
reserving parts she liked,
discarding bits she didn't,
trimming fat with knife.
She broke his bones and set them
in novel shapes that pleased her,
severed every heartstring
and wrapped them 'round her fingers.
And when the patchwork monster
still didn't fit her vision,
she scrapped the man that she, in vain,
had crafted in her image.
She sewed his lips shut like a corpse
and when he begged a chance,
she plucked her middle digit—
fuck you still made him dance.

One day Samson realized,
with locks growing anew,
he'd never liked his haircut—*she* did.
And she'd like it on the next man,
and the next man,
too.

-Andie Arlo

Chapter 3:

Haunted House

Is there a word for this?

The feeling when your landlord evicts you
nine months after your person dies;
says he wants to knock down your shitty house
and build two new ones in its place;
and he's an asshole
who's hassling you
about the damage deposit,
and in your grief you're primed for demolition,
but you stay standing;
and with every box you pack, you unpack,
say another goodbye
to another ghost
until you're infested with goodbyes
and ghosts;
and as you drive away, car crammed to the roof
so you can't look back in the rear-view,
you catch only the reflection
of vacant, wet eyes
and think,
there.
I did it.
I'm doing it.
I can do this on my own.

And then it punches you in the gut, because,
oh,
you never wanted to?

-Andie Arlo

Sarah AlNuaimi

Chapter 4:

Different Kinds of Ache

I'm not hurting. I am fine.
Loss is a given.
All my past selves are gone;
But maybe this picture,
held up to the sun
this song,
alone made of ice
this scent,
nutmeg and ginger
these flavors,
saffron,
cardamom
and spoonfuls of honey

will bring back some of what I've lost,
forgotten.

Destructive nostalgia;
now I'm cross-legged in the middle of dozens of shoe boxes,
filled with unprocessed negatives
and the hundreds of pictures scattered all around the floor—

None of which are with myself,
because I never really was present.
The S in *storm* is for Sarah,
always gone, always on the run.
It all went by so fast, like the glimpse of a shooting star,
gone in a blink.

I wish I knew better;
How to breathe,
how to stop and listen to the waves,
and no, flowers always made me sneeze.

Run. Breathe. Repeat.

Does the rhythm ever stop?
Inhale.
Exhale.
Every bargain has a price;
this time I'm paying double,
negotiating a deal I never signed up for
in the first place.
Stuck. Stuck in a rut.

"*Accept and don't you dare think it ends here.*"

It is *ache*.
It is what comes with the healing
that isn't linear,
isn't directional,
but a zigzag and an all over the place kinda hurt.
And so I keep falling back into the pain of anger,
anger,
anger and the oblivion
it brings along with it.

Different kinds of aches
ripping my heart to shreds.

-Sarah AlNuaimi

Chapter 5:

<u>Stages of Anguish</u>

the heart settling ache of breathing dust into my lungs
the pulsating all the way to the ends of my limbs
the tingling
the numbness
the sadness overtaking my thrill
choking me out of my words
eyes bursting with salt
a taste so familiar wets my lips
a sting
reminiscent agony
don't you just love it?

when I hurt in full color
high saturation
high contrast
nothing mute about my shades of red.

-Sarah AlNuaimi

About Sarah AlNuaimi

Sarah AlNuaimi (She/Her) is a writer from Ajman, United Arab Emirates. Sarah AlNuaimi is an Emirati writer, artist, photographer, coffee enthusiast and most recently a postcrosser (a person that sends postcards to strangers for other cards from other strangers on postcrossing.com). She's nuts for mail. When she is not receiving mail, she is sure the post office is conspiring against her. When she receives mail, she likes to head over to a coffee place on the way home and go on a date with all her postcards and letters. She is published in a poetry anthology titled Baring My Heart (Sail Publishing) in 2022. She likes hosting writing and painting workshops every now and then. She has a sixth sense and knows you're loving every bit of this book. You can find her on instagram @mail_bysan (if you ever want a postcard from her).

sarahaalnuaimi

Maya Averi

Chapter 6:

I Painted Myself as the Villain Before Anyone Else Ever Could

Rip it from their salacious mouths before they could register the taste
then smear the campaign across the walls
Call it immersion therapy
I will beat you at your own game
every fucking time
Silver tongues that split adjectives
with the precision of biochemists
Then spread them like butter across your mindset
You didn't create this feral beast, I did
Because the world is a stunning backdrop
but a motherfucker just the same
I wasn't going to let myself get swallowed
without a backup plan
I saw my giant heart coming, miles before
the sick and twisted did
Lightyears before she was led for the slaughter
like baby cattle

While dripping, drooling, hungry eyes try to compose themselves
in the presence of freshly fileted innocence
When "beautiful" things act up, no one knows why
Must be "broken"
The only thing broken is my silence
So, you'll have to excuse me while I slip into something
a little more volatile
Rage inducing
Worthy of hate
Fast talking
Slick mouthed
Heavy on the hard ass
Giving big bad monster vibes
If I've learned anything, it is not to apologize
for what I had to paint myself as
what I had to embody
just to survive

-Maya Averi

Chapter 7:

The World Asks for Honesty but Then Teaches You How to Be a Liar

A crash course
Omission
Stick your finger on the tip of a live flare, it's hot
White hot
Burn it twice and there's a scar
Scar tissue covers 90% of my body
It's emotional, not physical
Doesn't mean it's not there
I have fought wars over lifetimes
Put my weapons down long ago
Loss isn't a new thing to me
Grief isn't either
I move through both like it's a silent night
Secrets though…withholding—just like cash, burning holes in my pockets and tongue
Once a skilled collector of safe harboring truths
Only one tore right through me
The bayonet
I admire that soldier of a young girl though
The one whose father taught her: LOOSE LIPS SINK SHIPS
The one whose mother I still hear on the line constantly reminding
That I've always made my own path—again and again and again
Resourceful little survivor
There is peace in loneliness I think
When others' traumas nestle into the crooked bones that used to carry the
Unprocessed emotions of different lifetimes
Once you've stepped on those landmines,
You try not to put anyone else in that position
No man left behind they say
I guess you carve a spot, the structure gives way to the weight
No matter how carefully you dismantle your own bombs,
There are friendlies carrying grenade launchers just the same

I presume that it's easy to demand honor when your phantom limb
makes you feel like you're whole
When the sergeant screaming at you in the trenches has somehow lost
sight of the war
I presume that it's easy to see things in black and white when you're a
sharpshooter
Every fearful thought is suddenly a threat, and now a target
Except just because something lands in the crosshairs, doesn't mean
it should be shot
Cold wars never resolve quickly
And fear is the hair-trigger
I can negotiate a hostage but if we don't speak the same language
Am I doomed to be misunderstood?
Even in lack of understanding, one doesn't have to move to
waterboard
But that's the thing about the world—it asks for honesty
Then doesn't wait to hear the space between
Doesn't watch the queues
Picks out every other word and makes a mash-up
Then calls it truth
Black and white
That's the thing about the world—it only teaches you how to lie
I have fought wars over lifetimes
Put down my weapons long ago
If omission is my survival kit
I forfeit

-Maya Averi

Chapter 8:

The One Who Broke You Cannot Heal You

I've searched for answers in mouths that cradled lies with their
tongues
Saliva covered salvation rolling across tissued walls of withheld
validation
Never recognizing that a body that cannot hold truth
cannot offer peace
Or that a punctured heart, bleeds inner light
draining energy until you're dull
I've run after the taxi the way you've seen at the end of rom coms
heavy hearted, feeling that I'll drown without them
Refusing to see that they were never mine to hold
Some exits need to play out,
breaking me wide open
See the girl with the cracks, leaking love, bleeding light
See how much pain has taken over my insides
And I have tried
To find healing balm from hearts without eyes
Asking for band-aids in lieu of sutures
hoping for a stop gap
But things that are meant to stick, often don't
when faced with the warm, wet thickness of betrayal
Making any foundation hard to hold onto
I've surgically removed my backbone to make room for
large egos that operate like compactors
The ones that continue to demand more room
crushing the space I exist within, along with my confidence
Quickly forgetting how long it took me to find all the pieces
amongst the wreckage the last time
The truth is, you can survive crashes,
hope to find logic
pray for someone's mind to change,
beg for them to show up for you,
will it all to be different
You can lay yourself bare, attempting to be fully seen
You can stay far past expiration dates

Just to know…to be sure
As if you can't trust your own threshold for pain
As if your insides haven't liquified, or the whiplash has subsided
You can scream for a release
But harm and healing don't come from the same environment
Only one gives back,
Only one releases
Only one can set you free

-Maya Averi

About Maya Averi

Maya Averi (She/Her) is a writer from Chicago, IL. Fun fact: Once upon a time, her life goals consisted of becoming a "Fly Girl" on In Living Color (this was success in her book, you couldn't tell her it wasn't!) You can find her at mayaaveri.com

sincerelywithwords

Claire Bradbury

Chapter 9:

Wild Thing

I have been stagnant for too long
I let myself get caught up in the weeds
Let the vines take a hold of me
I wanted to be beautiful just for one moment
Wanted to belong to the earth
I wanted to live among the wildflowers

I forgot what it felt like to breathe
Forgot what it meant to be ever changing
I forgot I was not meant to be stuck in one place
I was never going to be a flower
I was meant to run wild through them

So I will pack up my things
I will leave this chapter behind me
I will pick the thorns out of my feet
Dust the cobwebs off my eyes

I remember now
Who I am meant to be
and a wild thing
is never meant for just one place

-Claire Bradbury

Chapter 10:

Devour

I will let this life devour me whole
I will break and burn
and dance even when there are tears
streaming down my face
I will love so fearlessly so fully
that by the time I am done
my heart will be shattered in pieces
The breaking will be painful
but the light that shines through
every single crack
will illuminate the whole world
I will hold your hand through it all
A single promise
That you will never have to spend
one single moment in the dark

-Claire Bradbury

Chapter 11:

<u>Legacy</u>

I plan to disappear for a while
I will pack a bag and go to Europe
Spend summers in the Italian countryside
I will sunbathe naked
Let every inch of my skin be kissed
by the Tuscan sun

I will throw my cell phone into the ocean in Portugal
Cancel every social media account I have
Grow out my hair and move to Spain
I will send past cards home
from every new city I go to

I will break my mother's heart softly
when I tell her I am never coming home
Deep down she knows she lost me
the moment my feet touched foreign ground
She will finally understand
She birthed a wild thing

When I turn 40 strangers and family
will finally stop asking if I am having children
They will never truly understand
that all of this was enough for me
One day someone will be walking down an old cobblestone street
They will walk into a dimly lit second hand book shop
Hidden underneath old leather bound books
They will come across a dusty book with my name on it
The only legacy I ever needed to leave behind

-Claire Bradbury

About Claire Bradbury

Claire Bradbury (She/Her) is a writer from Australia. Claire loves poetry as it allows her to express how she is feeling. It allows her to be vulnerable, open and honest with herself.

wanderingheartwords

Mariel Vanessa

Chapter 12:

Discord

I have dreamt in discord as of late.
Suffocated by the sounds
of unfamiliar towns,
tripping of gowns gathered
from the back of mother's closet.
"Darling, don't touch," but I am hard of hearing
and it is here that I fear
she has found all reason to run.
To flee, fledged in blood, she vows
to forget me by forest trees.
Made by the madness,
I am married off to man.
Bristled, fallen branches
break the skin of my feet,
I am told to meet him with a smile.
He is perturbed by a menacing grin
that prefers to unfurl tongue,
untie tissue, I tell him I am leaving
and never coming back.
Moored between two worlds,
all that is left are mistakes.
Mounted in a mausoleum next to memories
I don't remember.
My mind, a ransacked record shelf
I return to, only to yearn for mother's touch.
Perhaps I'd be wise to pick flowers
from another's garden
but this hardened heart beats violaceous scarred
for the monsters that grew in my own backyard.

-Mariel Vanessa

Chapter 13:

Missing Fate

You cannot force fate,
believe me, I've tried.
There are cracks in palms
of hands held tight.
A habitual breaking of skin,
I've collected drops of too much
blood. Timestamped and cultured,
I cannot bear to forget names and dates
of who decided to leave
and those I dared to stay.
Some say, fate
leads the willing. To where?
I'm not sure.
You see, my limbs are struck down
from leaving meaning on the lips of shiny things.
Sling bag straps snapped,
dragged by the weight of words.
Love appears overpriced and undervalued
and I have used every ounce of strength
to tie myself to weathervanes waiting
on the wind to show me the way.
I count cards in my favor
and pretend reversals don't exist
because I miss you,
miss us,
until I am the only one missing from this.

-Mariel Vanessa

Chapter 14:

Sound of Love

Confessions of love live at the back of my throat.
Trumpeted through consonants and vowels
and the syllabic sounds of "I love you"
spilled as haste from my mouth.
I wanted to convince you to stay.
Laying heads down in different cities
feels dismally cruel,
like a pocketed profession of hope that never reached you.
And you,
with those juniper eyes,
jumpstarting me by surprise,
I am arrested by the colors of green
that now make me cry,
I'd ask you why, but I already know.
Too late for a soul that stitched itself
to the underside of memories.
Do you remember building our forts on fantasy?
My mind, the muse,
your arms, the reverie
of every last daydream I couldn't leave behind.
Warring with time and the words
of songs seldom played,
where he wished she was closer
and she wished he had stayed.

-Mariel Vanessa

Caryn Clay

Chapter 15:

(untitled)

i tell you not to fall for me
(i don't mean it)
wonder if you can see the warning label it feels like i should come
with:
broken
in a scotch-taped up, peeling at the edges kind of way

i've never had a favorite anything
color
movie
song
is it too much to ask that even ordinary things take up residence under
my skin?

i look for reasons you shouldn't love me
unsure who i'm trying to make it easier on

being kissed in the rain is on the top of my bucket list

some days i'll be more in love with the moon, and
fuck
i need you to be too

i'll save the order sticker from a coffee you buy me because i like the
way your name looks in print

i'll copy words from your snaps and save them in a file on my phone,
so i have something of you when you leave

ask what you miss when you miss me
and when you say
it's the way i look at you, unfiltered and unguarded
i'll love and hate the truth in your answer

like i love and hate

that you know i can't stand the way my name sounds out loud, so you
only type 'C' when you tell me you love me

i'll wrap my leg around yours while kissing you naked in the kitchen
and when you lift me up,
i'll rest my bare foot on the back of your calf
falling in love with the way it fits

i'll tell you you're the ocean and the sky and poetry

get off to the sound of you telling me you love me
nevermind that it's only playing in my head
(sometimes i pick at the scotch tape)

i'll wonder if you ever shower just to feel the burn?
dial turned all the way to the left
fire on your skin
air thick enough that it has to be consumed rather than simply
breathed

i love the same way

-Caryn Clay

Chapter 16:

(untitled)

sometimes we're crowded rooms
stolen glances
your eyes like melted chocolate
the kind you suck slowly off fingertips
the kind that lead to backseats
elevators
hiked skirts worn on purpose

sometimes we're restaurants in NOLA
keys to an apartment we never rented
(the one you were 90% sure of)
i can still smell the pour over in the kitchen
as i sit at a familiar table that isn't familiar at all
reading a book full of blank pages

do you remember that time you pulled me into a stairwell?
the way we echoed
a reminder to passers-by that life is short
too short.
in the same way that *my skin is too soft*
my body feels too good
and *you want me too much*

maybe i shouldn't, but i like when we give in
become all sweat.
hands.
nerve endings.
masks set aside.
fists full of sheets.
a whispered *yes* in my ear as you arch my back and sink yourself into
me

this is the part where i tell you *i love you too much*
(you don't correct me)

so instead, i pledge myself to you with every moan you pull from my body
you're the only one i cum for
you're the only one i come for

i know love is a word we try not to say
like the cigarettes i try not to pick up
too easy to fall back into
so i put it out.
remove the 'we' from between my fingers
shake the sleep from my eyes
(unsure which is memory and which is dream)
let the embers fade into my mind and wonder
if you'll ever let me bring you back to burning

-Caryn Clay

Chapter 17:

(untitled)

you pull me into you
tilt my chin up
make my mouth your mouth

sometimes it stops there
a quick exchange of soul
a reminder that we can still feel things

but tonight.
tonight
buttons slip from holes.
straps fall from shoulders.
i feel my back press against the wall
and your hand become fingers

soft at first.
as many times as we've been here
we still go into it like it's the first and last time

your eyes search mine
asking a question you already know the answer to.
yours

grips tighten
fingertips dig into thighs
teeth make butterfly bite marks out of shoulder blades
and i whisper what sounds like a prayer
god.
don't.
stop.

you don't.
and i smell like you.
and i smell like you.
'no expectations' i remind myself out loud

as i search my skin for another hit
(fuck)
i smell like you

-Caryn Clay

Chapter 18:

(untitled)

i feel more ghost than flesh these days
more bruise than bone
'tired' has morphed into something that i look up synonyms for.
new ways to tell my friends the same thing

exhausted.
worn out.
drained.

i'm hungry.
the kind of hungry that makes my chest ache like it's been hollowed
out with a butter knife
the kind that makes my head spin and fog at the same time
a hungry that makes my mouth water involuntarily
(god, that's so fucking annoying)

it's never made sense to me how the lack of something can make you
want to vomit up your insides.
i drink coffee instead
(insert whatever you like here
i do)

jaded.
burnt out.
shattered.

i tell myself it helps
convince myself the frostbite settling in behind my rib cage will thaw
if i can just make it to spring

fatigued.
enervated.
run down.

there's this sweater that i wear all the time

it's completely falling apart
nothing particularly sentimental about it
it doesn't even keep me warm
and i can't remember the last time it did

still i reach for it
refuse to throw it away
a part of me needs to believe you don't have to get rid of things just
because they have holes in them

weary.
broken-down.
depleted.
done.

-Caryn Clay

About Caryn Clay

Caryn Clay (She/Her) is a writer in Louisiana. She never wears matching socks.

coffee.poems.repeat

Lindsay Arbuckle Courcelle

Chapter 19:

<u>I Dreamt of You Again</u>

But this time you weren't a scared little girl
Hungry and cold
Abandoned
In that dark house in the woods

You were a lifeless baby
Clutched tightly in my arms

I struggled as I wandered on a college campus
Trying to find a way out
Down many stairs in a crowded auditorium
Almost dropping you

Until finally
I found an exit
But it was an elevator that compressed us
I did all I could to resist it
To keep it from crushing you

And when we escaped
You blurred into my boy
Full of life and energy
And it was no longer a college
But an amusement park
My son put his soft hand in mine
And led me playfully onward

I want you to know
I think of you often
I dream of you
I weep for you
And I love you

I've let go of my shame
And guilt

And I wish you well
And I'll honor you
Wherever you are
For all my days

-Lindsay Arbuckle Courcelle

Chapter 20:

<u>Too Happy</u>

I worry I'm too happy to write a poem

But then
My little raccoon
wants to snuggle with me
In his cozy den
Blankets bundling up our love

My daughter brushes her own hair
And I see how each day
She blooms in her beauty

The first frost
White meadow below
Leaves shining their colors
Blue sky smiling at me

A kiss from my husband
His loving presence
As he looks deep into me
Asks how I feel
On this morning
In this moment

And I tell him
"I feel so happy."

And I know
This is enough
For a poem.

-Lindsay Arbuckle Courcelle

Chapter 21:

22

Only a gardener like you could tend to a plant like me.

My early days
Were as a seed
Blowing in the wind
For many years
Touching down
But never rooting
Into the deep Earth

Over Kansas prairies I flew
And all of the West
To the Puget Sound
And through the jungles of Ecuador
And finally
Finally
I landed on the coast of Maine
And my hull cracked open

The first roots sipping water from the sandy soil
Cotyledons drawing in the ocean air
Beating heart finding its song again
Dancing on the beach alone
My 23rd birthday
Tears salty like the sea
And I knew magic had germinated

At times the solid ground
Of our 92 acres
Of lush Vermont green
Of our sacred union
Feel as foreign to my roots
As the South Pacific
As concrete sidewalks
As plastic pots

These days
These days
I want to float into the sky
Like the fluffy seed I once was
Until I hit a fast current
And ride the wind like a sandhill crane

For years I did not migrate
For years I let my roots grow deep
Snaking their way
To the molten lava core
Bringing the fire up into my soul
The warmth into my heart center
But the seed memory remained
In one tiny cell
Of one tiny petal

Then this petal
Just this one
Was plucked out by a child
Who used it in a potion
Who made magic from my pain
This alchemy
This transmutation of memory
Of trauma
It healed me deeply

Four amaranth sprouted in our kitchen garden
Three together
One alone

Only a gardener like you
With your knowing hands
Your intuition
And your heart like mycelium through the soil
Could dig up the one lone flower
Gently, without breaking her roots
Tenderly, without causing her stress
Without any damage whatsoever
And plant her with her family

And it couldn't be this way
Without all the oxygen
All the raindrops
All the magic
Gathered from all the corners of the sky

Now, she can root.
Now, she can grow.
Now, she blooms.

-Lindsay Arbuckle Courcelle

About Lindsay Arbuckle Courcelle

Lindsay Courcelle (She/Her) is a writer from Vermont. Poetry allows the creative forces of the Universe to flow through her pelvis and heart and onto the paper. You can find her at alchemymfr.com

[O] alchemymfr

Noemi D.

Chapter 22:

For My Sister

(Trigger Warning: Sexual Assault, Suicide)

I spoke to her in subtle solidarity
seven years too late.
She let me slip over the details I had forgotten to ask for.
In what world do we exist where I am grateful to hear the words, "he
only beat me" fall from my sister's lips like bloodied knees to the
ground?
In first grade Mickey with the brown eyes used to push me as hard as
he could
and I would smile because that meant he liked me more than my best
friend Megen.
Those are the stories I can talk about.

Plagued by haunting dreams I asked a therapist once to help me find
clarity
in the shadows of my childhood.
She told me my mind was protecting me from things it wasn't ready
to process.
I was comforted by that fog,
a warm blanket around me, so I stopped trying to figure out
which nightmares were real.
Those are the stories we don't talk about.

One day, over a bottle of wine,
I will tell my sister how at 15, I was high and drunk and Brian
climbed on top of me and how for 15 more years I hated myself for
only telling him no and not screaming it because I didn't want his
parents to hear.
I didn't know that night would cost me whole relationships, that I
would sacrifice my softness to win every fight no matter what was
lost,
because when it mattered most, I wasn't strong enough.
I will tell her over the second bottle how he licked my face and
laughed, and how the stain of his breath on my skin has never left me.

A few years ago I saw a Facebook post offering condolences to his family after
he had driven his car into a building, stumbled from the wreckage and slashed
his own neck open with pieces of broken glass.
His death didn't bring me the peace I thought it would.
Just more violence
and more silence
when friends wrote about
what a good man he was.
And these are the stories I can talk about.

In the poem I will never write, I will tell my sister how when I was 17,
I ended up in a hotel room with a 23-year-old man, how he made me
shower with him after and how it was that part that made me sick inside.
I will tell her how six weeks later I had an abortion that I have never once regretted.
I hope she will say that 17 is a child and not a guilt sentence,
that all the years I spent blaming the taste of my own skin,
my blackberry lipstick,
my wet and wild eyes,
that those too were not his to take.

Maybe she will tell me her own stories
of how I was born by the ocean, and she was born in the forest,
and we both gave too much light to men whose shadows crippled us,
and how still we don't know home.

I have outgrown shame.
I have outgrown the desperate need to know which monsters of my
childhood were real, because it will still just be something I can't talk about
something I survived
on the surface.
In what world do we exist, where that is enough?

-Noemi D.

Chapter 23:

Love Letter to Yourself

do not feel pity for the man who sleeps at the foot of the bed you have cast him out of
though every bone, every muscle fiber in you longs to comfort the ache in him
even as you sit alone in yours

you have been here before
your body knows both sides of this california king
knows one day you will understand this betrayal is a gift
knows that the part of you that wants to heal the hands that hurt you
is only the ghost of your childhood
is only an eight-year-old girl trying to forgive her father for the unforgivable

let her go
your broken heart will wait patiently
there are worse things than loneliness
do not give any more of your ribs to the wolves
so sad in their hunger
so desperate in their pain that you would carve out your insides
feed them from the palm of your hand
watch the drops of your blood spill heavy and red
while you starve quietly
do not be uncomfortable in the empty space
instead hold the silence, wrap the stillness around you
know that winter is coming
and that you have survived a thousand cold mornings before and after him

skip the anger
you are not 29 and full of things to throw
you are beauty in the deluge
you are grace in the devastation
remember it was always women who carried you
who pushed breath into drowning lungs

who brought life into the dead places

dream of your mother
who has been here too
dream that you are with her at a station that should feel familiar but
doesn't
you are trying to find your way home but
the map is a circus of colored lines and numbers
you can't find the right train
you step on then off one, then another, just as the doors close
you begin to panic
you look over and she is laughing
she is stronger than you remembered
the dream ends
she is not afraid
you are not afraid

-Noemi D.

About Noemi D.

Noemi (She/Her) is a writer from the Bay to LA. She comes from women who speak without speaking, they gave her their words. You can find her on her website at whatbeautifuldisaster.wordpress.com

[O] whatbeautifuldisaster_

Katarzyna Dąbrowska

Chapter 24:

(Untitled)

I don't want to start this by telling you
that you are wrong but you, my dear,
are in fact wrong.

My walls might be built up solid,
high and strong,
but confusing that with
a lack of tenderness would be a mistake.

(Yo, there is a moat, didn't you see?)

You're also wrong
about us not being aligned.
Unless you have met someone else.
Because in that case,
the lack of alignment isn't due to a lack of tenderness.

I can get mad real quick and I snap;
I'm working on it.
You run and hide.
That's our damage.
I can work with yours if you will work with mine.

My tenderness is in how I make coffee
and cook breakfast.
It's how I would stroke your hair,
or hold your face before I lean in to kiss you.

I dose it out, tenderly checking
if it's safe to take the next step.

I projected onto you past fears and hurts,
I put you in the same category
as one of the worst human beings
that ever lived in the history of the world.

And I'm sorry. For that my heart hurts.

We don't have a foundation yet
to be able to deal with each other delicately.

When you said what you said, my body argued.
I felt myself double over in pain and wailed.
A reaction of a wounded animal.

I don't want to walk this off.

I want to know what your skin smells like
when it's been out in the sun.
I want to know what it feels like
to curl up next to you in bed.
I want to know what it feels like
to sit in your lap and fold into you.
I want answers to all the questions
I wrote down in my notebook to ask you later.

It would suck if there wasn't a later,
because I was really looking forward to later.
That's all the tenderness I have for you.

Tennyson out.

-Katarzyna Dąbrowska

Chapter 25:

(untitled)

I'm not looking for a pen pal
to exchange occasional nothings with
I already have pen pals
who I exchange everythings with
You and I
are not the same
I'm in the mosh pit of a concert
I'm at an ayahuasca ceremony
I'm holding my friend's hair while she pukes into the ocean
I'm running from the cops
You're at home procrastinating
Your mortal existence is a shame
And your higher self is crying
Begging you to live
Because while you spend your life getting imaginary ducks in a row
Pretending that one day
You will be enough
To live
To love
To create
I'm living a million lives
In one day
So
Boy
Bye
See you never

-Katarzyna Dąbrowska

Chapter 26:

(untitled)

He came to my funeral
I never knew who told him
His love and friendship ancient, like him
4,553 years old
Face weathered, still beautiful as ever
Saying "Black might not crack but beige doesn't age honey and don't
you forget it"
He wore a black wide brimmed hat
Perfectly tailored suit
Diamond earrings

An oak in a primordial forest
Burning sweet candles and spiced incense
Praying to the moon
Wishing me well

Every time he thinks of me he still smiles

He tries to tell me that the anger I hold onto only hurts me
He's not wrong, sometimes

I'm just a little bit mad, still
And I don't know if I'm ever not going to be just a little bit mad

It's lighter though, knowing
His ancestors stand behind me
Offering divine protection
Part of the tribe forever

I built a monument the last time his soul left this realm
A past life
So the world wouldn't forget

To this day
A lighthouse stands next to a pyramid

A beautiful mosaic
The inscription of a husband whose heart is still wrung by
insurmountable grief

They tore down the cross
A symbol of something long buried
And no longer of itself

Like Jesus

-Katarzyna Dąbrowska

About Katarzyna Dabrowski

Katarzyna Dabrowski is a Polish author from the Gold Coast Australia, who likes to skip countries and start new lives.

wwkadd

Paula Dixon

Chapter 27:

Leaving the Cage

I place my face inches from the fan,
Whisper my spells.
The spinning disrupts, distorts my voice.
Magnifies its magic.
I am tempted to place my finger between the too wide,
Not safe for children
Gaps in the twisted metal cage.
I have been spared before from near death.
Surely, I would escape the biting teeth.
My work is not finished.
I cannot be destroyed.
Yet.

Regardless of my intense belief in my invincibility,
I become careful.
Begin forming my own cage,
Mirroring the twisted metal surrounding the fan.
I slice my hands with the work.
Develop calluses as I continue.
Piece by piece fashioning the bars
Into the finest examples of devil's rope,
Carefully placed, magnificent barbs.

My banshee spirit howls at her confinement,
And I will not free her.
Determined to excel,
My name on every honor roll,
Go to a fine Christian college,
Choose a respected profession,
Follow the dress code,
Skirts no more than two inches above the knees,
Tucked, tied, combed.

My inner demon threatens to end us both.
Sacrifice our life for her liberty.

I collect more strips,
Twist and turn them to fill the empty spaces,
Create the most beautiful, gilded cage.
I feel the burn as my fire signs consume me from my core.
Fed by the unholy wraith that inhabits my flesh.
The light reaches the hollow of my long dead eyes.
The blaze now beyond my control.
Fiery tongues lick through my outer shell,
Smoke and heat fill the container.
The harpy's cackle rings.
We must exit the cell or perish here on its floor.

I will break my own arms, if necessary
To peel apart the layers of exquisite metal.
They will no longer decorate the wild spirit inside me,
Hold her captive to society's ideals.
I break out,
Spy signal fires of all the others,
Destroying their own cages.
Eye the abyss,
Swallow
My
Fear.
Join the host of other beings
With fire-stained wings.

-Paula Dixon

Chapter 28:

Star Dust

When my circle was at its smallest I did not know.
I imagined it a wide, wild place,
Filled to its brim
With adventure
And chaos.
I knew in time
My circle would cross
With that of my prince,
My savior,
Who would carry
To his world,
Free from the circles of rage
That pulsed through mine.

I could not know
My prince would prefer skirts
And tiaras,
Be leery of the dark,
Carry fear in a thermos
That should have held life-giving water.
I did not know
She would be prone to running.
I did not know
My prince would be me,
Continually changing the size of our circle,
Expanding, contracting,
Including, excluding.
Compacting our joy, our sorrow,
Our everything.
Only to explode
A supernova
Spewing out bits into the universe,
Gambling on being seen,
Gathered up like so many specks of stardust on foreign planets,
Set in jars among other stars.

-Paula Dixon

Chapter 29:

Love Letter

I am bare feet
Dancing across worn wooden floors
In a slip of a dress,
Belting out Johnny Cash,
"I walk the line."
Preparing breakfast
On our second-hand stove
With only three working eyes,
And one of those with only two settings,
Off and hell.
Bright red coils suitable for boiling water,
And charring everything else.
The sun peaks over the ridge
Shines in her first rays
Through the dusty window.
I breathe a prayer of thanksgiving
That we set the kitchen facing due east.
Eggs hit the oil
A hiss, a sizzle
One flip
And they are just my way
Firm whites,
A middle that will ooze as I slice it.
Hot black coffee,
A side of buttered toast,
And it is the best love letter I have ever written.

-Paula Dixon

About Paula Dixon

Paula Dixon (She/Her) is a writer from Georgia, USA. She takes pretty pictures. Does not write pretty poems.

[instagram] music_poetry_pics

Malialani Dullanty

Chapter 30

I Used to be Worse

I used to be worse.
No really.
I used to be like her,
the one you can't even begin
to say the name of.
I used to be like him,
the one who still
makes your hand clench into a fist.
Even after all this time,
as if time would be enough.
And yet,
it was for me.

I used to be worse.
No really.
Steal your boyfriend,
kiss your girlfriend,
manipulate my way in,
lie my way out,
point the finger
any direction except toward me.
Until I
finally did.

I used to be worse.
No really.
But still
I'm standing here,
on the edge of always,
telling you softly, firmly, kindly
I used to be worse.
Maybe it's an excuse,
maybe I'm not really any better,
but that's not what I said,
is it, darling?
I just want you to know,
I used to be worse.

-Malialani Dullanty

Chapter 31:

Secrets

"Tell me a secret," I whisper
late in the night, I don't want
a n y t h i n g   e l s e.
Like they're my currency,
like they're my love language.
I don't want your touch or your time
or your presents or your acts of service
- I want your vulnerability.
I want secrets whispered to me as we
lay in bed, fingers, legs, hearts intertwined -
or, rather, splayed out wide, laid bare
in front of me
so I can tell if you're safe for me
to do the same.
And I won't hold them against you,
no,
not even the ones you think are darkest.
not even the ones that are hard to speak aloud.
And it's okay if you've told them
to someone else
before.
It's okay.
It's okay.
It's okay.
It's just that they're answer
and I'm asking -
see, I'm asking,
if you could love me.

-Malialani Dullanty

Chapter 32:

How to Breathe

I'm not breathing,
my body is doing it for me and
gods
gods
gods
isn't it beautiful?

On the playground in early summer,
still breathing.
Behind stage right in the dark,
still breathing.
Stomach full of charcoal,
still breathing.
Plates flying,
still breathing.
Collapsed on the shower floor
too sticky with too much blood,
still breathing.
Lying on the cold tile,
still breathing.
Drug addled,
still breathing.
Heartbroken,
still breathing.

Still.
Breathing.

These beautiful lungs breathing
all on their own,
until I remembered how.

-Malialani Dullanty

About Malialani Dullanty

Malialani Dullanty (She/Her) is a writer from Hawaii. Writing is freedom embodied. You can find her at malialanimade.com

[O] malialani

Pascaline Dussaut

Chapter 33:

In Another Life

In another life I meet you when we're 14 years old

I meet you before the drugs do
It takes you two hours to fall in love with me
So. very. madly. in love!

Less friends, no weed
Just your sport…and me!

In another life I come to all your matches
I'm louder than any cheerleader
I scream your name from the top of every stadium
And you never give up on playing
Just so you can hear my voice scream your name.

In another life we're 15
You covered the floor of your bedroom with candles
Your mom is out of town for business
And we make love for the first time
In another life your kisses feel like velvet on my skin
There's blood on the blue sheets
You're sweating
And you look at me and tell me you love me
It smells like something is burning
We jump off the bed, the curtains are on fire.
And in another life our naked bodies throw buckets of water on the
flames
And we laugh
and we laugh so much

In another life you get a scholarship
In another life you become a professional athlete
In another life you are dedicated to your health
And I fly to Europe and I sing opera

In another life we break up
And I turn on my computer to see your face at times

I don't see you for three years until that trip to Istanbul
This city feels so familiar
The Bosphorus reminds me of you for some reason I can't really comprehend
In another life it's 11 o'clock, I'm walking down a park filled with tulips
I'm facing the water and there you are.
Sitting on a bench watching the fishermen

In another life my heart is about to come out of my chest
I sit on the bench and say "Hi"
We fall into each other's arms
And never let go again.
Never.

In another life we are inseparable
Machu Picchu, mushrooms in Amsterdam, Karaoke in Tokyo, Bahamas and its pigs
in the water, we ski in the Alps, deltaplanes in Switzerland, art in Venice,
so many concerts in Paris, so many football matches in the US,
we dance so often, a house in California, four kids, you build me a studio
where I sing and paint and have sex with you every single week.

In another life your lungs are clear
Your words are soft
You love walking
Cherish nature
You're an aries, so honest and loyal
In another life I know you honor me in every detail.

In another life when we're old
When our knees hurt
We still write love notes on the bathroom mirrors
We still make love in the shower
We still laugh at the burned curtains we couldn't hide from your mom
In another life we take french classes together
We drive up highway 1 thirty six times just to camp between the sequoias.

In another life you wake up in the morning
You look at my wrinkled face

You touch my white hair and tell me I'm beautiful

In another life we die together
They never find our bodies
They are too deep in the Pacific Ocean
They'll say we had a car accident
But our kids know we drove off the cliff on purpose

They found a note on our bed
"This one was beautiful and now your dad and I are ready to find
each other all over again in another life"

-Pascaline Dussaut

Chapter 34:

<u>April Snow</u>

You could have left me in the jungle
I would have survived and mastered bird language
Adaptability is my secret weapon.

I was that kid who danced and screamed out of joy
when the tropical rain hit the tin roof of my house.

I had renamed myself April Snow.
My dad had made me a bow and arrows that killed a big spider one
day.
I was playing with knives and fire, my feet were red from the soil.
I told my sorrows to a tree
My skin was tan, my hair was long
I ran faster than the boys…
And bragged about it.

I was singing in a language I didn't understand
The ocean fascinated me, soft shades of blue, dangerous fish and
sharp corals.
I swam.

My mom made us climb a volcano
A freaking volcano!
This woman never got the credit she deserves
My mother is a shy and humble…Force

I pulled hermit crabs out of their shells, put them on my hook
and went fishing with my dad
How? How is this me?

What happened?

I settled in a gigantic concrete mess
Did I get trapped? Not really…
Was his bed too comfortable that I gave my bow and arrows away?

Was the food too abundant that I stopped fishing?

Or was it my dream? I know she needs a big city but still…
My biggest phobia is sharks now! I don't swim anymore.

And the tropical rain, the ukulele…I miss them…
Oh I miss them!

I know this little girl, April Snow, lives in me.
I feel her when I sing foreign words,
when I play with cameras and put paint on canvases.
I know she helped me through my divorce and reminded me that a pretty house
is useless when you can't be yourself in it.
When my babies need protection she snaps out of her nap, and she's right here, Savage ready to attack.

I laugh in disbelief but she wants to jump at his throat when he calls me degenerate.

I know she lives in me.
This life I created, it hypnotizes her like a snake.
She's half asleep most of the time and I know it's only up to me to wake her up.
So wake her!
Kill the snake, eat it and use its skin to make yourself a ring
Embrace her and all her fierceness, her imagination and all that freedom she breathes.
All that freedom.

-Pascaline Dussaut

Chapter 35:

Istanbul

I'm a bad lover
You've been there for me for 14 years now
That's 5110 days of you choosing me over and over
Making me stay.

I'm a bad lover
I talk shit about you
I tell people you're messier than me
So disorganized!
I complain about how you treat women sometimes
I say you're loud,
You act like if you don't like the color green,
Less and less trees
You don't look after your dog properly
And you have more cats than my grandma ever had
Her whole life!

I'm a bad lover
I screamed at you so many times, telling you to let me go.
People ask me how life is with you
Judgemental smiles on their faces,
A little afraid, they ask me.
Your people ask the question: "Why? Why do you stay?"

You see…I didn't choose you
It was destiny

And eventually I left it all, for you.
Was it your blue eyes?
And this promise I was going to be protected
Or was it your blue heart?
All this water in you

You are very welcoming.
You held me like I was yours from the very beginning

Calling me 'canim'…'my soul'
You taught me a new language
You made me the best breakfasts
You gave me friends…so many friends.
You even gave me confidence in myself
You look at me like if I'm different…and special

You see…I may complain about you but I notice the good you did for
me.
I am grateful for it all.

Should I mention how dramatic you are?
How fiery.
And yet so tolerant and so kind
(Except when you drive)
You're just like your flag,
Intense red…passion
Soft white crescent and its sweet star in the middle

I'm a bad lover
I fought with you so many times.
I stepped on your name,
Slammed the door at your face yelling:
"I'm done, we're done, I'm leaving now"
You ran after me, each time!
And embraced me even tighter whispering to my heart:
"I choose you, I choose you, I choose you"

I know you love me just the way I am
I know you want me in your arms.
But I'm not sure you know how I feel about you
So here it is:
"I love you Istanbul…Forever"

-Pascaline Dussaut

Amanda Dzimianski

Chapter 36:

Word Me a Bridge

word me a bridge
across the chasm
from where I am
to where the language
and line
breaks
build a better world

carve me out
a clock
unsullied by time-keeping
cracking cosmic code
for climbing out past the edges
of over-consciousness

draw me a dimension
in which I can
hurry my pen
across a kind page
undistracted
by the demons
in my mind
whispering my wanting-ness
my failures of the future
pre-imagined in vivid
nightmare glow

let me place my body
on the end
of that crackling line
straining
to receive through the static
recording the dispatches
from within
the voice willing

to whisper all the secrets awake

liberate me
from that tight-lipped fear
side-eyeing me the threat
that free flow
will forever elude me

they say all kinds of things
about 'appointments'
or the brisk walk
but Imposter's my girl
and she knows—

write it and it just might
bite
back
slap me across the face
with too much of me
and all I can't make
and how I know the way
but not how to say it

-Amanda Dzimianski

Chapter 37:

On Sacrifice

i could sing down the moon for you
fling a rope around a star
and yank it from the sky
i could unbury all the treasure
lay it out in the light to sparkle
and burn all the ships
i could meld our souls as one
melt the metals enfolded in flesh
and fuse them solid

i could

but I won't
because adding in
perfect harmony
will only ever equal
subtraction
from symphonic score
for us
and i refuse to lose myself
for less
than the music
we already make

-Amanda Dzimianski

Chapter 38:

Transference

i torch the cord
twining her to me
the golden woman
twice-incarnated
evil-twinned too long

smoke from our burned edges
gently spirals, withers upward
contrasting the wrench away of the wraith
an un-self unfettered

there's something of a death rattle
in the exhale

what never belonged here snatched back
receding into coffin-velvet horizon

and i can see the water now
pristine and free-form and enough

the pines pierce the star-scattered veil over me
a warm wind winds itself around my limbs
and everything is mine

i steal from no one
leave no space of absence
receive from abundance, never lack

i feel the stone beneath my shoe-shed feet
smooth
firm
fixed
my hands palm the surface of this rock

and i am my own

the sovereign's robe silkens down from my shoulders
while the moon keeps vigil with me and i light
another fire, forging friendship with the land
and there is nothing more to fear

all the flames are mine

because mine
is my kingdom
and my power
and my story
forever

-Amanda Dzimianski

About Amanda Dzimianski

Amanda Dzimianksi (She/Her/Hers) is a writer from Athens, GA, home of the Yuchi, Muscogee/Creek, and Cherokee (Eastern) peoples. For her, Starcrossed Poetry has been a safe place to be more of her snow-on-the-beach self. She is incredibly grateful. You can find her at amandadzimianski.com

amanda.idareyoutospellit

Allie Evans

Chapter 39:

(untitled)

The fragility of the world economy is exposed.
Societal pillars now show their persistent cracks.
But they always existed.
Hidden.

Webs of international markets stretched too tight.
Intensifying tensions building in all the backgrounds.
How do we explain this quiet chaos to the boomers?
They worked so hard to build this dreamland.
For us.
For each generation to live better than the previous.
Improvement equated to receiving what we want,
When we want it.
Just in time.

Global capitalism continues to shape our desires,
Producing all the items we believe we need to survive.
Globalization was not only a buzzword invented in the 90s.
This subjugation always existed.
Raping the land of all its resources.
Built upon centuries of exploration and colonial expansion.

Many forget that they still have a choice.
Daily we are faced with vital choices.
Most actively choose to continue participating in the game.
The ongoing construction of the dream.
The centuries-old dream of our ancestors,
Created by mazes of economical transactions,
That took centuries to create,
And decades to perfect.

It has always been fragile.
Barely sufficing the clockwork of increasing pressures.
Until the wheel recently broke.
The momentum stumbled,

And now fails to recover.
The effects are surfacing.

Many are still oblivious to the inevitable changes,
Demanding we stay on the same comfortable course.
But the good-hearted heroes are tired.
They have used up all the elbow grease available,
Until resilience and brute strength are not enough.
Perseverance is turning into a weakness,
And acclimatization needs to be celebrated.
If there is ever a time to reach deep inside your soul,
To extract your superpower,
The time is now.

Nearing the endgame,
Faces make the motions to cry,
But no tears fall.
Will we be witnesses to the great fall?
The worldwide heaviness is real.
Life only seems too heavy if we don't want to accept the changes
taking place.
That means if it feels too heavy,
Use it as your sign that you must adapt now,
Before it is too late.

-Allie Evans

Chapter 40:

(untitled)

yes, love.
you can be whomever you want to be.
fantasy is not just for movies and fairytales,
it is for a life worth living.

the story starts when youth and wisdom juxtapose without being a
dichotomy.
then one day, and there will be a day, you forget who you are.
you morph into exactly what you think is necessary to survive.
you will succeed.
the success might haunt you.

but don't be sad,
you will always find her waiting for your return.
she will be on the playroom floor with open arms.
asking you if you want to play army men or legos.

she will give you insight to your past.
she will remind you of the lessons you already learned.
she will be your friend.
she is always your best friend,
and that is why you return.

someday, you'll decide to stay.
you'll finally realize,
that you already had everything you needed on that playroom floor.
with arms wide open she waited.
a playmate.
a confidant.
with army men
and legos.

-Allie Evans

(untitled)

Focus on the forces of gold,
And illuminate the hidden truths.
Follow the path beyond the gate,
But don't forget to shut it securely behind you.
The five piles of pine needles were yours alone to find.
Step out of the spinning wheel of houses by trusting your wings.
The realm of strength needs not just brute force,
But a reminder that gentle truths can be harder to handle and tougher
to stomach.
Don't be sidetracked by the simple pests,
They are only a distraction planted in the way,
To show you which doors not to enter.
You don't need to express factual anger right now.
Just live your life. Be you.
This is the work you actually need to do.
Take these golden opportunities to awaken yourself,
And to progressively awaken the rest of them.
They are ready.
Hello, we are here.

-Allie Evans

About Allie Evans

Allie Evans (She/Her) is a writer from Bellingham, WA. For continued transformation, Allie believes we have to get our thoughts out of our body and connect with a like-minded community to promote these transformations.

 Allie.in.flow

Josie Fuller

Chapter 42:

<u>Vines</u>

I wonder when the southern live oak
begins to notice
its own suffocation
if it can feel the thick vines of ivy
slowly creeping forth
while the light begins to dim

does it even matter
if it cannot run?

my grandmother
was a beautiful socialite
in 1940s Miami
with the face of a movie star
she sparkled
like a purple gem dahlia
after a splendid wedding
she was plucked from her cherished ground
and replanted
in a tiny Everglades sugar mill town
where life was filled
with slow creeping vines
her light dimmed
under the clutches of responsibility
routine
restraint

it might be her voice I hear
when I feel the ivy creeping
and picture the kudzu-strangled woods
of my childhood in Atlanta
her voice
telling me not to get tangled
to run from the mundane
reminding me

that I have the luxury
of conscious choice
that my only cage
is of my own construction

while she
was an amethyst starling
with iridescent violet feathers
wings clipped
a cocktail in her grasp,
the insidious liquid memento
of a glittering past life
fading from view

a tree covered in ivy
can stand for decades
and still thrive
like a drowning woman
clings to her very own vines
to survive

-Josie Fuller

Chapter 43:

Self Portrait

Where loneliness cracks like lightning
I'm a storm over open plain

I'm a fire blazing swiftly through lush, ripe fields
of South Florida sugarcane

I'm a flash of green against damp, dark earth
a promise, soon to bloom

I'm a bright flicker of candlelight in the corner
giving life to a darkened room

I'm a steady voice across canyons
a hidden strength amid the great unknown

I'm a heartwarming hand bringing comfort
as it clasps my very own

I'm a wild wind whistling, a force with each breath,
up against the Sycamore tree

Yet for a moment I could have sworn
I heard myself whisper,

Who will be strong for me?

-Josie Fuller

Chapter 44:

Empty Space

maybe you mourn

what they cannot give to you
and an empty space within
grows cavernous,
hungry
oh how you try to fill it
numb it
outrun it

maybe if you pour yourself into others
they'll pour back into you
(they don't)
maybe every decade
you become another person's scapegoat
after overdosing on their toxicity
maybe you find relief
when you stumble upon
the   very   last   fucking   straw

for it is then you finally see
how that hollow place
has pushed and pulled you,
with its subtle message
of unworthiness,
to search for yourself
in the eyes of the world
crying out at every turn
"who am I to YOU?"

maybe
you ask the Grand Canyon
how her emptiness
feels so very full

maybe you trek her rugged ridges
journey down past 80 million years
and there in her barren embrace
there, amidst everything and nothing

you find your own empty space
just as wildly spectacular

-Josie Fuller

About Josie Fuller

Josie Fuller (She/Her) is a writer from North Carolina.

📷 josiane.poetry

Stacey Gibbins

Chapter 45:

(untitled)

(Trigger Warning: Abuse)

It is easy to say if I had chosen differently, my life would have been better. It is easy to compare stories, watch friends' lives unfold, and witness the contrast at arm's length while choosing to be a victim of circumstance. It takes work to confront your shadows and generational patterns. It is difficult to bear witness to the deeply entangled wounds that keep oneself and many others in their victimhood. Every one of us, in our way, releases wounds from one generation to the next. And some barrel down the falls, head first, trying to dismantle it all. We are:

•The black sheep.

•The cycle breakers.
•The ugly ducklings.

The annoying thorn that does not disappear.
We are steadfast in our commitment not to be *the same* while stumbling and tumbling to realize that we are *the same*.

They will stop and stare and say, *why are you this way? Why can't you handle it or get over it? Why do you need attention? Validation? We are tired of your dramatic storytelling.* And I will say *because I can.* I can be vulnerable and brave and lean into the pain and hurt because I no longer want to hold this shame. And so, with one deep breath, my swan song unfolds—the end to a beginning.

Had I never chosen,
I would have never experienced words as stones
I would have never experienced feeling unlovable
I would have never experienced flipped tables, and holes in the walls
I would have never experienced compressed vocal cords
I would have never experienced being thrown up the stairs
I would have never experienced uncontrollable hatred

I would have never experienced wishing for death
I would not have made myself fit into compartmental boxes
I would not have created and worn so many masks
I would not have said, "it is okay" when it was not okay
I would not have said yes when I truly meant no
I would not have chipped away at my soul, believing everyone who ripped at my core
I would not have had to lose myself over and over to simply be
I would not have had to choose to be different so that I could heal

I could have screamed and cursed out in vain
I could have outwardly told anyone what I didn't like about them while strategically hating myself more
I could have cut off my sisters, serenading everyone with my victimhood
I could have chosen to cleanse myself within my addictions (vodka-infused spite)
I could have never taken accountability, burying my head in the sand
I could have chosen to deepen my wounds and their infliction on others
I could have chosen all of these and more had my wise ancestors never knocked on my door
They said to me, no more believing these lies;
That everything I accomplish is tied to my worth
The way I look is a direct correlation to how I am to be loved
That loyalty is staying and taking all the abuse, and in relation, I am safe

Because I chose,
I know true love
I know the presence of a big family
I know the flavors that embody generations in my recipes today
I know the power of a diverse music catalog
I know the true meaning of resilience
I know the peace in simplicity
I know genuine full-belly laughter

I dream of peace and grace and more time together
I dream of Friday night dance parties
I dream of our growing family mirroring healing wisdom
I dream of watching my kids and nieces and nephews chasing butterflies
and capturing grasshoppers in old mason jars like I did as a kid
I dream of my family being joy-filled and holistically healthy
I dream of having all of us living on a big country plot, growing old(er)

I dream of new memories that heal old wounds

I am my mother and father's daughter
I am called to do this work, and I know I am not alone
I am the straw and the camel
I am trying and failing
I am love and pain
I am light and I am darkness
I am all things, and so are you
My ancestors said to me,
It is time to let go
To unchain yourself from protection, from control
Your words are to be known
Only then will you experience the beauty to unfold

-Stacey Gibbins

Chapter 46:

(untitled)

my soul began to scream
a visceral
guttural roar
my chest burst into porcupines
i ripped out my vocal cords
and God, she R O A R E D
I AM DONE
i showered
i put on my yoga pants
laced up my kicks
ran my fingers through my messy bun
sports bra and t-shirt in hand
i took a deep breathe
and greeted the outside
b r e a t h e in
breathe o u t
a path made with each step
a plan in motion
i bleached and cleaned his entire space
leave no trace
i packed up all my shit and left
no note
no goodbye
just hot tears on the fourth of July
screaming with fear and pride

-Stacey Gibbins

Chapter 47:

Bath & Lace

(in a clawfoot amongst the ancient trees)
she splays
steeped in golden honeysuckle
baby's breath perched atop her crown
dripping in viridescent lace
petals arousing as she hums
barefaced and unadorned
milky water surrounding her breast
in a faint whisper, *she hears*
goddess, what is your muse?
she takes a sip of her wine
rolling the notes on her tongue
a descant purses her lips
me.

-Stacey Gibbins

Nargis Hassanali

Chapter 48:

(untitled)

We all have something or the other in life that we cannot have or get despite loving it strength lies in letting go then loving

-Nargis Hassanali

Chapter 49:

(untitled)

I felt so confined within my surroundings, at one point I was exhausted so I burst opened myself into flames of colors like the wings of a butterfly and flew higher

-Nargis Hassanali

Chapter 50:

(untitled)

I went from wanting to be a writer, to a pilot, to a psychologist, to a nutritionist and finally a teacher. Today I asked myself the same question and my heart whispered an architect, so I could build a home in my body so I am never a stranger to myself

-Nargis Hassanali

About Nargis Hassanali

Nargis Hassanali (She/Her) is a writer from Dar-es-salaam, Tanzania. She started writing poetry in 2013. Nargis picked up a pen one day and wrote down everything she was feeling. For Nargis, it felt so good to release everything that she had been holding inside. She has continued to write and has found it to be a great healing process.

[O] nargis_shabbir_hassanali

Bryttney Huseas

Chapter 51:

(untitled)

what is it
to be a mother

if not
to protect
to lavish love
to endlessly wish good things
for your precious ones

what if i
were
also
a precious one

continuously expanding & giving birth
feeding with my very body
bleeding heart
forever present & kind
for
my
precious one

-Bryttney Huseas

Chapter 52:

(untitled)

I want to be known for how my hair blows in the wind
    how the green and yellow in my eyes shimmer in golden hour
    how I sway in my hammock and get lost in the sky
    how I shake my body all around the house
    when I am too cooped up throughout the day
    how my laugh bubbles up and explodes—touching everything
    surrounding
    how when I finally soften—anything can make me tear up
    how I love being soft
    how I long to make you feel special although I am not the best at
    planning ahead
    how I make matcha chais with lemon cake (& would love for
    you to join)
    how I look you in the eyes and see you
    how I devoted my life to loving myself wholeheartedly

-Bryttney Huseas

Chapter 53:

(untitled)

I do not wish to domesticate you

I wish to enthrone you

All the while
You spill a drink
Rip your clothes

Looking at me
Awaiting my response

I gasp!
At the delectable goodness
The utter perfection
Of your recklessness

Not only the cliche of wild thing
But feral to your core

Increasing in excitement
Your mouthiness results in someone getting bit

A little blood never really hurt anyone

-Bryttney Huseas

About Bryttney Huseas

Bryttney Huseas (She/Her) is a writer from Tempe, AZ. For Bryttney, writing means diving into her internal world and helping it surface, express & flow.

 bhuze

Melissa Ives

Chapter 54:

Ghosts

In this push and pull
I don't know how
to NOT love you
Leaving love notes
drawing names in the sand
Facing the wind and the sea
Professing my love and all that you are to me
I am ok knowing we can't be together
I am not ok when I start to question why
The what ifs creep in
The made up happy ending
The one where we stay together
And then I remember why
You don't want me
I am loving a ghost
You don't reach for me
Take pics of me
Mention me in any post
But today you wore the Mala beads
You see, I am in everything
I am petting the dog at the end of the photo
I am just to the side of every mountain video
You remember, the one you took on my birthday
Strategically cropping me out
And then saying it was unintentional
How could I not know?
How could I not see
The ghost was never you
You made the ghost
Me

-Melissa Ives

Alexandra Giffin

Chapter 55

Earth Ships

Taste of dusk is on our lips
clouds corral the setting sun,
The Sangre de Cristo's lapping lilac skies
like a hungry dog on the hunt

earth ships adorn the desert landscape
radiating our recycled dreams,
because nothing feels more like freedom
than our feet planted on wild ground

And what will we find in comfort,
other than our wandering souls?
Aching in their wantonness,
dreaming of their own vibrant colors

The canyon lands point the way,
teasing our curiosity
with snake bends and jagged skeletons,
another chance to make right our wrongs

I could have touched you then,
I would have touched you then...

But some journeys are not among the earth,
and the wind won't always tell us the way—
We are not what we have become,
we are not our yesterdays

So let the humming canyon
erode our persistent pace,
let the mountain hymns
teach us their ancient alchemy—

So when we lay beneath an endless sky
we will know...

The desert breathes as we do
and blood flows through our veins
just as the snaking river
rushes toward her imminent lover

Now darkness blankets fragmented thoughts
with a crushed velvet blue,
may we sleep one more dreamless night
may we wake embracing our truth

I could have touched you then,
I would have touched you then…

But some journeys are not among the earth,
and the wind won't always tell us the way—
We are not what we have become,
we are not our yesterdays.

-Alexandra Giffin

Chapter 56:

October Sky

I felt the vastness
of your absence
like the sky in October—
when I found your letters
at the foot of my bed,
and the sun streamed across the walls while I read them.
The room sparkled
with glimmers of your memory,
and for a moment I thought
the light would stay…
Oh, how often we suffer
in our own resistance to change.
I find solace in the shadows
of these walls
as I sift through my loneliness,
uncomfortable at times
with the weight of letting go—
how home,
once a sturdy place
now erased
with a longing
for belonging
to myself again.
Graced by the pace
of a shifting season,
finding reason
in the gifts of slowing down—
as the nights grow longer,
and the wind a bit colder,
I'm filled with wonder
at the rhythm of time,
which both grief and nature
suffer no bind.
I owe nothing to these years
but lines on my face,

and in between
this pendulum swing,
I find I still have so much to give.
The October sun is setting
while the trees dance
with twilight—
delicately dressed
in gold and green,
I can't help but think of you
when the leaves begin to fall—
so proudly it seems,
in their last goodbye.

-Alexandra Giffin

Chapter 57:

Seasons

True beauty is found
in a collision of earth and bones,
a melding and alchemy
of all that remains unknown—

And only if we are brave
can we walk that glorious path,
wearing a patchwork of forgiveness,
bearing a heart made out of glass.

So let us love the endings
as much as our beginnings,
because true wisdom is found
in the frayed edges of our bindings,

filling in blank pages
with words of a common thread,
tethered and tangled in weighty roots
that bind to supple skin—

seasons that weathered us,
and washed away
what might have been—
not giving up,
just
giving
in.

-Alexandra Giffin

About Alexandra Giffin

Alexandra Giffin (She/Her) is a writer from Glacier, WA. Alexandra draws inspiration from nature to connect more deeply with her own seasons of life. Her poetry reflects on themes of love and loss; contrasting human experiences with the rhythms and cycles of the earth. Originally from Colorado, she now resides with her husband and dog in the Pacific Northwest, tucked into the beautiful Cascade mountains near Mt. Baker, Washington.

 xelalive.

Samantha Prasad

Chapter 58:

Hello

Hello to speckled sand and the sound of a griddle
slathered in pancake batter—extra chocolate chips.
Hello to the sea on my eyelashes.
To country music constantly playing—pop, too.
To stacks of vinyl records and piles of books—in every corner, on
every shelf.
Hello to healing, resonating, expanding, manifesting.

Hello to wholesome.

Hello to dancing in the kitchen.
To jumping on the bed—ruining the mattress in more ways than one.
Hello to happy lumps in my throat.

To sandpaper kisses from the cat.
To wet ones from the dogs.

Hello to new running trails and the smell of sassafras and Dame's
Rocket.
Hello to afternoons lounging in hammocks, sprawled in the sunshine.
To never too many candles—sandalwood, eucalyptus, Moroccan
amber, wild mint. Hello to traipsing across the globe.
To Santorini, the Amalfi Coast, Croatia, Kenya.
To every single nook and cranny.

Hello to new people. Strangers turned friends turned family.

Hello to my reflection.
Hello to admiring myself, to loving myself.

Hello to learning new words—*erlebnisse, nepenthe, alpas, kairos*.

Hello to full bellies, swollen hearts.
Hello to that feeling that I deserve all of this and more.

Hello to grabbing it, keeping it, welcoming it.
Take a seat, make yourself comfortable.
Stay awhile.
Stay forever.

-Samantha Prasad

Chapter 59:

B.F.

I read somewhere that the chances of us meeting were .0001%,
like odds can define friendship and love.
On a planet of random soulmates, in a universe of binary spinning
stars, it took one conference room, a panel interview, and a handshake
to find familiarity.
Coworkers first, friends second, lovers later.
Lifetimes before; lifetimes to go.

Did I feel an immediate sense of ease around you? Absolutely.
But nothing more than a friendly face,
a fellow human that would wander through nature with me.

Statistically speaking, I had permanently placed you in my friend
group.
We did not lock eyes, there were no stolen glances.
There were lunches and syrup stains and "we are paying separately."

But then what came over you that one March afternoon,
languid legs after our 20-mile hike.
"What do I do, with these feelings for you?"

It is not often I am rendered speechless, but render me you did.
Now what am I to do with all of this waiting?
All of this wanting — should I let this happen to me?
I don't want to be a footnote in your story.
I used to be innocent. I am now wild.

"I will love you forever."

Well fuck, me too — I will stand on this high ledge and love you
forever.
Because I am wild, I am free, I choose this. I choose you.
However unlikely, we are here. Us. You. Yes. Always.

How does one measure the length of yearning anyway?

Can you hold forever in the space where two hands meet?
The odds were against us — March to August, cradling anguish in a
sling.
Heartache is a chapter, at least.

But falling in love—
Well, falling in love can add up to the whole fucking thing.

-Samantha Prasad

Chapter 60:

(Untitled)

My horoscope tells me my heart has wild edges,
like I read them for any other reason than to reaffirm what I already
know.

That I can be too much—
ask for too much,
demand too much.

Because most of my life I was never too much.
I was tiny, small—
Invisible.
With a capital fucking "I".

I listened.
I pleased.
I satisfied.

So quiet,
the golden child,

what a good little girl.

And then…
and then.

I kicked a hole through the door of my childhood bedroom.
I combined some disgusting peach vodka with a handful of
Trazodone.
I stopped sticking my tongue between my teeth and said *fuck* out
loud.

I climbed up an Indonesian volcano in the middle of the night,
with a flashlight so delicate it fit in the palm of my hand.

I ran into the Pacific Ocean fully clothed,
dunked my head in seven times.
I read long, long ago, that's what Naaman did.
Into the Jordan, to heal his sickness.

Anything to drown the depression.
(It worked, for the record.)

I made my exile an exodus.
The great homecoming,
of a heart so ablaze
it could only fit into the chest of a woman on fire.

-Samantha Prasad

About Samantha Prasad

Samantha (Sam) Prasad, (She/Her/Hers), is a writer from California. For Sam, poetry serves as a way to heal, to imagine, to forgive, to transcend, to love. Outside of writing, Sam keeps herself busy with exploring running trails, discovering new bookstores and coffee shops, and working as both a digital marketer and sexual assault counselor.

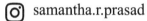 samantha.r.prasad

Shannon Reilly-Yael

Chapter 61:

The Weaning

You have no memory now of
their lives before the milk.
It's been three years, your breasts have gone
from incidental coverings to
the things she knows are love.

Remember when you had to stand your ground behind them,
insist your presence against the crumbling wall of yourself?
When they tumbled down more and more milk from a hidden source
so mysterious you could only know it as yourself, you began to trust
them
for the first time, smiled down at them like the heads of two extra
children,
gifts you'd never expected.

Womanhood had come to you during the night,
that fairy who lands like a shimmering midwife upon the nipples:
at ten, puckering them into strange buttons that necessitated veiling,
then shaping them into mounds the let rise too long
before returning to set the oven.

When heartbeat of the fetus began, you stopped
vomiting woozily each morning and gaze
at their darkened nipples browned into the same shade
all mother-nipples come to with their purpose.

When the end is near, you know well the fairy who whispers them
back into your body as though they are beached whales needing to be
reminded of the sea, the freedom of hiddenness.

-Shannon Reilly-Yael

Chapter 62:

<u>Bangles</u>

breezeless on the rope bed
we leaned on our limbs
revealed our skin
to a stillness stirred
by flies

with my nails
painted
blood red

cheap

by the neighbor
sashi
in the red and gold sari

we resembled a harem
it was so hot the polish had not dried
choomaloo blew
at fingers and flies

the doors and windows
opened wide
then you
in the doorframe
leisurely returning
to take possession

padma wakes
to make you
one chai
with swiftness
from scratch

we relinquish the bed

but you beckon me back
frown at my nails
have chinee smear red off
carefully
with her lungee
wet with kerosene

from brown paper
you produce
glass bangles
red ones
you look hard at my face
take my hand
bend the bones
to the point of snapping
work glass
over joints
along skin

relentlessly

until my arms feel like
freshly skinned snakes
bound by a circumference
of danger, exposed
to the precariousness
of glass offered
as a gift

i cannot refuse
and i thank you
but

i cannot lean on my forearms
i jingle wherever i go
announce myself like
the whirring fly
somersaulting bongo beats
into glass encasement

my hindu refinements
exasperate my inclination
to imitate silence and i
plot my escape
recruit the neighbor
to restore me

untraditional
again

i end up bangled
unable to be free
unless a man
strong as he
bent me
backwards

agreed

now whenever i see
broken bangles
glinting out from dust
i remember
gritting my teeth,
taking aim
at the stone wall
the sound of the
tinkle of shards of glass
sent sailing
into the sacred river
as i shrieked
and i shiver.

-Shannon Reilly-Yael

Chapter 63:

Sun Prairie

When I think of death, I only
regret that I will not be able to
see this beautiful country
anymore... unless the Indians
are right and my spirit will walk
here after I'm gone.
Georgia O'Keefe

Who would have known
from the photograph with its
careful hues of shadow,
its dark absence of color

that you painted flowers
bright and bold in red
and yellow shone on
by the prairie sun,
layered skirts of
flamenco dancers
touched by your brush
while you dreamed of stars?

The wings you wore rested
while your eyes looked beyond
the window at the wisdom
you would find yourself
wrinkled into as an old woman
living on the ranch of ghosts.

Some silent-flying creature lurked
in your face then. She would embark
on flights over frosty dawn fields,
exposing her armpits to the cold,
stirring the air with quiet dreams
before the sun rose, when she would

perch in a dark hollow, huddled
against the heat with closed eyes,
dreaming the dreams of the coldest
moment of night collected under
her downy wing feathers speckled
symmetrical as twin sisters' freckles,
breathing her cold air and its soft
strokes of dawn into the light.

-Shannon Reilly-Yael

Chapter 64:

<u>Stun and Awe</u>

I wish Monica was
George's type.
She could negotiate
world peace,
disappear below his desk,
undo the bible belt with her teeth.

Oh Monica, where are you
to bend and suck
the most insensate member of
the American monarchy?

With your gentle mouth,
inveigle his virgulate
Bush
towards peace.

Pacify him pleased,
and make flaccid
his viagric obsession
with preemptive ejaculation.

His instinct for destruction is inherited:
he needs exhibitionism.
Monica, will you please
give George a blowjob?

-Shannon Reilly-Yael

About Shannon Reilly-Yael

Shannon Reilly-Yael (She/They) is a writer from Vancouver Island, Canada. Starcrossed poetry community is unconditional community support.

Ⓞ Epicwomyn

Katie Riley

Chapter 65

We All Believe in the Same God

We all believe in the same god
The rings of a tree mirror my fingerprint
And if you look deep into my mind
You will see the universe before you
That same one
As old a fantasy as time

Dwarf pitch pines cones are opened by wildfire
Destruction breathes again and germinates
Black spruce makes sap to protect me
So my blood clots to protect her
Does entrust their fawns to front porches
And there are legends of orphans raised by wolves
We each are borne from the ribs of another

Have you ever pulled a carrot from the ground?
In the ancient city of pasta and stone
My wine drunk craving was zucchini
Flames danced before me once
And I watched them burn

Laundry is strung out the window and it's mine
Yet it dances the melody
Of generations of women before me
I
don't
come from this land but it doesn't matter
I carry them in me

Every year flowers bloom
Every year flowers bloom!
And every year I'll gladly bake and burn
Beneath the sun
Because how different are we really?
(Just like any medicine

Too much will surely kill me
Perhaps I am an addict after all)

Who of us has not found enough fish
In desperation?
Who has not opened her mouth
And breathed fire?
Found answers in the silence after a storm?

The craziest part is the debate
Of who is right
And who is wrong
As if we are not all singing the same song

-Katie Riley

Chapter 66

Woman Weeps

Woman weeps
And weeps and weeps
Her tears reach around the world
Drops from eyes of blue and brown
Meet
To fill the deepest crack in the planet
Where no man has ever been
Where did you think the salt came from?

In seventh grade I learned
Dihydrogen monoxide is eternally recycled
Every drop has always been.
Cleopatra's sweat streaks my cheeks
Wets my lips
Rains on my wedding day

The warrior's widow mourns
Her cries carve the Grand Canyon
She jumps.

Woman weeps
And weeps and weeps
Her tears feed the oceans
Her moon tugs the tides

Until, at last! She's had enough.
Deep below the surface
A rumble
A quake
The lava in her body melts her chains
And erupts
Forcing a ten-story wave!
The tears of Mary and Rosa and Jane and
Malala and Frida and Maya and me
Desolate

Demand to be seen

For too long
We've fed the oceans

Woman weeps
And weeps and weeps
Sea levels rise
After ten thousand years we've had
Enough.
One can only surmise
The rhythmic 'plink'
Of the tears we cry
Will be your final lullaby

For too long we've fed the oceans

-Katie Riley

Chapter 67:

Fixes

(Trigger Warning: Substance Use, Death)

If I could bottle
The sun shining through autumn fog
Soft burning branches
An empty highway
I'd drink myself dead

If I could crystallize
Sunrise hope and sunset youth
I'd give it my last breath

I'd scrape sweet pine
Into thin white lines
On the stillness of a clear lake sky

And only from cold gray hands
Could you pry
A summit-sharp syringe
Of crunchy leaves and whipping wind
Which grows its roots
Up creeks of blue
Beneath my stardust
Skin

-Katie Riley

Chapter 68:

<u>Equinox</u>

Autumn blew in on a rain cloud
And thus the season of falling leaves
Began with falling water
And a symphony
Of droplets splattering pavement

Reminders of the beauty of
letting
things
go
"Things" you thought you needed to breathe
"Things" that turn sunlight into sustenance

Until suddenly
You remember
You've been standing tall for a hundred years
Your bark is tough
You have seasons of stores within you
Your roots run deep
Your leaves will return in the spring
Not to mention
You've done this all before
And grown taller
Stronger
Greater
Each season

-Katie Riley

About Katie Riley

Katie Riley (She/Her) is a writer from New Paltz, NY. Katie is a yoga teacher, social worker, and traveler. As a lifelong creative, poetry is her way of painting her experiences through words.

[O] katieerileyy

Michelle Shaffner

Chapter 69:

Main

Neither of us want tapas,
small bites of manchego, jamón.
We want the wide brim,
paella coloring the pan,
beady-eyed shrimp, saffron,
rice sticking to the side of the steel.
We want to be savored,
felt in the belly,
full with one another,
drinking Roussanne
from one another's palms,
crema catalana licked from our wrists.
Secrets.
If, somehow,
I was in a sudden accident, Impaled:
Kahlo—
Broadsided:
Gaudi—
I'm afraid poetry
would come spilling out of me, a tangled river,
gnarling, teeth bared,
Or maybe just like…
A dam, broken,
telling secrets,
scribbles on paper,
pieces of your handwriting and my heart.

-Michelle Shaffner

Chapter 70:

Drawers

(After Mary Oliver: Wild Geese)
Written to Nuvole Bianche: Ludovico Einaudi

Whoever you are,
you do not have to live blindly,
day through day,
humming a numbing song.
You only have to believe
that what you feel,
what is hidden, tucked away
in the drawers of your lungs,
your breath, in and out by the second, is worth pulling out.
Worth living through.
And loving through.
And fucking through.
And goddamn hurting through.
Tell me about
that which is tucked away for you. That which you long for.
Love for.
Fuck for.
Hurt for.
Believe
that what you thought you'd left,
that which is still haunting your bones, that which sits
unsettled in the small of your back, behind your eyes,
scratching your spine,
is worth facing.
It is.
Whoever you are,
know it will hurt.
It will cut deep.
It is not kind.

But it will open you how you've longed to be opened.
It will open you how
you need to be opened.
It has opened me how I needed to be opened.

-Michelle Shaffner

About Michelle Shaffner

Michelle Shaffner (She/Her) is a writer from Minneapolis, MN. Michelle is a dreamer, a connector, an optimist, a learner, and a lover. She lives in Minneapolis, Minnesota, with her husband and two boys. When she's not writing, she teaches English and enjoys cabin and sauna life. She also plays old punk songs on the ukulele and is the most ardent John Prine fan in her family.

Shahd Thani

Chapter 71:

Quarantine Chronicles

There is a playlist of you and I.
A record of a life we created in one another.
The first coffee run when my hand brushed yours,
the first embrace of tangled fingers,
your lips on mine, gentle and all encompassing.
The songs we danced to on a deserted beach
with no one to witness it but the sunrise.
The long drives where we belt out the words
at the top of our lungs and steal furtive looks
at one another. I still remember the euphoria
of falling, falling, into your arms.
We burn brighter together like a bonfire
and this remains a manifesto of every moment
we ever loved out loud.
Now the hours are so long, days blending into
one another, a Groundhog's Day we relive over and over
and you are here, but not really here. Long distance love
stretched across neighborhoods and I'm yearning
for all the things we took for granted.
The hot bread we shared and how you always
let me have the last bite of cake. The warmth of
your knee against mine as you pass me a plate.
It's not the postcard-perfect
moments that I miss the most, but life as it unfolded.
The whispers, eyes locking across a table,
and the easy way our shoulders brushed one another.
Those ordinary moments are what I treasure the most.

I miss you ~~being less than 6 feet away from me.~~

I miss you being a breath apart from me.

-Shahd Thani

Chapter 72:

<u>Lanterns and Snowglobes</u>

I still write you postcards I'll never send
Lighting up all the runway lights to guide you home
And trying to forget all the planes are slumbering now

I still write you postcards I'll never send
Scared that I have faded into Sepia tones
While you are high-definition color

Do you remember falling in love in Tokyo?
Your hand in mine, under pink clouds
Cherry blossom petals falling like snow

It seems so long ago now
A waking dream, a burning memory
Did I dream you into life?

It's snowing in Tokyo today and I wonder
If snowflakes on Sakura feel like kisses
falling around us like glitter in a snow globe

Your hand was in mine, luxurious warmth
Heat wrapping around my heart
Strolling underneath the pink lanterns

When the the sun set casting everything
In golden hues, I felt so alive
Basking in your gaze

We used to be magic within a snow globe
We're outside it now, palms against cold glass
My soul searching for yours in the darkness

Do you still light lanterns for me?

-Shahd Thani

Chapter 73:

Is Anybody Listening?

I'm falling apart in the dark. What a recipe for disaster?
I'm drowning in the deluge of memories.
Pandora's box coming undone; faded cinema tickets,
Dried petals, birthday cards, your perfume rising
Like a ghost, a decade later and it still feels like an embrace.

Is anybody listening? Is anybody there?

Maybe I'm playing with fire trying to find you
in the social media sphere. Tweeting songs
we used to listen to. Taking photos of the cafes we loved.
I'm buying bouquets of sunflowers because you always
said you liked how I held sunshine in my arms.

Is anybody listening? Is anybody there?

Will I find pieces of myself in your eyes?
The crumpled promises we gave each other.
Does it even matter anymore?
I loved you once. I love you still

Are you still here? Are you listening?

I'm packing up the memories again
I'm wiping the tears again.
I hope nobody heard.

Fuck, I hope you aren't listening.

-Shahd Thani

About Shahd Thani

Shahd Thani (She/Her) is a writer from Dubai, United Arab Emirates. She is an Emirati romance writer and poet. She is passionate about love and aspires to be the one reading bedtime stories, romances, and the occasional menu on Audible. Her proudest accomplishment in the Starcrossed community has been hosting the Meet Cute and Other First Workshop and loves the serendipity of being published with the Starcrossed community in this anthology. She is published in an anthology called Dear Future Lover 2023 as well as a collection of poetry titled Fields of Poetry (Sail Publishing) in 2021. She won the Emirates Literature Mentorship Award in 2016.

 shahdthani

Sarah Elizabeth Van Syckel

Chapter 74:

I Am Not Ready to Die Yet

after Joy Harjo

(Trigger Warning: Death, Illness)

Death sits next to me in the sterile
infusion room
Takes a bite of his cheeseburger
sips his milkshake
tells me to fight it
He likes watching the game
Red Devil charges on ahead sword
at the ready
Clumsy, destroying anything and everything
in his path and
I think he'll take all of me.
But I am not ready to die yet
and despite the benadryl drip dream
I tell Death I'll buy him a bacon dog when I win.

That night as I gently drag my fingers
swirling, up and down
my body, around my breasts committing
to memory the way it feels to be
touched, there
the full moon goddesses light
dances across my skin
tells me my story.
Lovers and almost lovers
Her touch, his hands
reminding me I am alive.

I named my depression long ago
Roxanne
We meet often, I take her to the lake

wander the woodlands
Show her the growth
green rising
She would rather shrink
But I am not ready to die yet.

So we continue to fight, as I promised
hand in hand
Even as cancer takes pieces of me and my spirit
wanes takes me to the bluff whispers *I can't anymore*,
but I do.

The waves crash below me, angry and ready
to devour me
I step back, fall into a soft bed of wildflowers
use my hands to bring me back
to myself, remember how his tongue, teeth felt
tasting and tugging I can feel it again
I will feel again
Before Death returns.

When his horse arrives, we will toast our
whiskies,
share a pizza and watch the rain fall
chat about how I beat him
all those years ago and tore the cancer
cell by cell from my body
how I burned down my whole fucking world
rose from the ashes
walked out of the flames
billowing plume leading sisters
reborn warriors eternal

-Sarah Elizabeth Van Syckel

Chapter 75:

Wild reclaiming

I'm trying too hard
Drinking coffee barefoot in the grass
grounding
holy.
I used to think god was speaking to me
whenever I saw a rainbow
'Everything will be ok'
Today there is a woman in the clouds
Soft, powerful, ever-changing.
Humans can find meaning in anything.

Queen of Cups told me to connect
to my intuition, to write from that place.
I reach past my ribs
open me up
take my hands and scoop out all my insides
until I am laid bare.
Religion took my gut from me
Taught me to distrust myself
I choke on it
Can't tell me from them.

Of course you are an extension of
the world that told me I am no good
not enough
too much
You are small
Thieved my wild
I have been stripped to the bone
Let the dogs in.
Little did I know
tearing the flesh from my body
excavating
I'd find myself
Underneath

In the muck
string me back together
messy
magnificent
mighty

Goddess.
I want to be worshipped
Bring me your sacrifice
Make it bloody
Make it something you love
bring me nostalgia
Lay it at my alter
Swoon when I sing Jewel after we make love
Motorcycle rumble
between my thighs
awakened
wild.

-Sarah Elizabeth Van Syckel

Chapter 76:

Muse

sometimes i wish i had a muse.
she is free and open and sees
into the deepest chasms of me.
maybe she laughs and lifts
her face to the sky and opens
her arms wide every time she witnesses
the sun setting. as if she has never been more delighted
by anything else in her whole fucking life.
maybe she teaches me how to
salsa in the kitchen. maybe we
stay up all night talking about
our fears and dreams and mistakes
and deepest desires. maybe she teaches me
how to make love. maybe her hands
heal every wound inside of me,
open and scarred, known and
unknown. maybe all of our broken pieces
fit together like a stained glass window.
maybe i write about how she moves like
water, gentle, refreshing, but weathering,
smoothing my rough edges.
maybe i write about how she makes me laugh.
how her compassion and ability to see others pain
is one of the million little things i love about her.
maybe she breaks me wide open.
maybe i am her.
muse and writer and healer and my own fucking hero
and epic love.

-Sarah Elizabeth Van Syckel

About Sarah Elizabeth Van Syckel

Sarah Van Syckel (She/Her) is a writer from Dingmans Ferry, PA. As soon as she could read, Sarah's grandfather started having her recite poetry. She distinctly remembers reading Elizabeth Barrett Browning's "How Do I Love Thee?" in his office, where she spent a great deal of time after school. Writing, poetry specifically, became Sarah's way of making sense of the world and processing her experiences. You can find her at sarahvansyckel.com

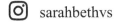 sarahbethvs

Ioana Varga

Chapter 77

I Want to Write a Poem About Queer Joy

(Trigger Warning: Homophobia, Death)

but the thing is
they keep killing us
guns
and laws
and pointed fingers sharp as blades
love unbound
spilling crimson down sidewalks painted rainbow for clout
i want to write a poem about queer joy
all kiss-swollen smiles
and a dining table big enough for a crowd
about all the things truer than the aim of a bullet
forget that they'd rather see us dead
than dancing
i want to say *look!*
sometimes truth doesn't end in tragedy
i want to write a poem about queer joy
to talk about my friend
who thinks there's nothing romantic about loving off-script
if it puts you in an early grave
how he loves anyway
a love that cracks him wide open
about community
and locked arms
and how, when we make it
not for a single second
not ever
do we forget the many who didn't
i want to write a poem about queer joy
a poem that's not an obituary
but liberation
dripping from my lips
pumping in my chest
to remember that they might have claws and fangs and armies but we

we have something they can't take away
this is my favorite intersection in vienna
with the seven tram stops and
the old walnut trees and
the smelly greek restaurant
where we said goodbye for the very last time
it was may and you were moving to rome and i had no idea how to
tell you not to go
because i hadn't yet figured out how to love women like you bright
and tender and loud
courageous like a storm in july
so i swallowed the poem, said
'i hope the apartment search goes well'
fingers bleeding
blue nail polish falling into a cold cup of coffee you pulled your hair
up
ebony curls at your temples, said
'here's to new beginnings friend, come visit'
it's winter now
i sleep next to a man who loves me well
and knows me little
the leaves of the walnut trees have all fallen
i still wear blue polish
keep my fingernails short

i think of september
right before the red truck took you away
i almost bought the plane tickets
i almost picked up the phone
i almost made it

you've left
before i could type it all out
i will forever have
almost
loved you

-Ioana Varga

About Ioana Varga

Ioana Varga (She/Her) is a writer from Vienna, Austria. Ioana writes poetry as a reminder that she is here, we are here, that we are deliciously and painfully alive. She writes poetry because it's what remains when she feels like she has nothing else. Ioana writes poetry because she is mostly introverted and it's the best way she knows to reach out a hand.

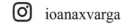 ioanaxvarga

Holly Webb

Chapter 78

Mother Nature Is a Lover Like No Other

I want the ocean to fuck me gloriously
Crashing into me along the shoreline
Scratches up my back from the shells and sand
Sea foam finding the pressure points on my neck
Seaweed tying my hands down as the ocean has its way with me
And I welcome it, gasping
Water licking open the oyster between my legs finding the treasure,
the shiniest pearl
The water kisses from my jaw to my knee and says goodbye, the tide
going out
I get up, weak-kneed and know that I am charged on a molecular
level.
Salt water runs through my veins now, not blood
The ocean claimed me as its own and
I know
That was my purpose

-Holly Webb

Chapter 79:

That Mr. And Mrs. Smith Kind of Love

I want to be so in love we're trashing hotel rooms
Drop your coffee cup on the floor to kiss me
Push the lamp off so you can eat me out on the desk
Drag me by my ankles to the edge of the bed
Rip down the curtains as you press me up against the window
Fingertips cracking the mirror as you bend me over the sink
Too busy kissing and knocking shit over
Too busy howling into one another's mouths
Ripping sheets
Breaking shit
Cracking headboards
Tangling limbs
I want us to be so obsessed with each other
That we
Break the cups
Break the table
Break the headboards
Fuck it all
So we can fuck on it all

-Holly Webb

Chapter 80

Praxidice Incarnate

I am vengeance
Pussy dripping blood
Not from the moon
But the cycle of ripping to shreds
Any dick that enters it
I will tear you to fucking pieces
And never confess the sin
I am karma, bitch,
And karma is a bitch, bitch
I am the baseball bat
Taken to heads of rapists
I am the harpies
Three sisters in one body
The fates bow to me,
Because I decide who deserves to live
And whose string deserves to be cut.
I don't pray to karma,
Karma prays to me.

-Holly Webb

About Holly Webb

Holly Amber Webb (She/They) is a writer from NYC, NY. To her, poetry is the rawest expression of feeling. Poetry on paper is what dance is to the body. Both reading and writing poetry has helped me through so much in my life, and I couldn't imagine my life without it. This anthology is sacred. It's a culmination of artists from all walks of life who are coming together to create something just as powerful and unique as we are. I am honored to be a part of Starcrossed Community and a part of this anthology. I'm so excited for what's to come. You can find her at https://hollyamberwebb.wixsite.com/author

[Instagram] Authorhollyamberwebb

Jen Wieber

Chapter 81

Jar 328

He walked into the prayer room
that night after dinner.

Tentative
but hopeful.

They gathered around him,
kneeling,
and one of women
rested her sweaty hand
on his shoulder. She prayed
loudly.

Too loudly.

She prayed with gumption that his colon
would unwrap itself and give this man
relief from his pain.

In Jesus' name.

Her hand felt hot enough
to burn a hole in his shirt.

She went on a couple more
sentences, about this vision
she received when
one of the elders leaned over and
loudly whispered,
"He had his colon removed
when he was just a boy."

Oh, she stammered.
As she stopped talking
altogether.

Thankfully.

And therein began the
disconcerting dreams.
The ones that showed
his extracted intestines,
having been squished
inside jar 328,
waking up suddenly
to unfurl itself
out of its knotted misery
in the basement laboratory
room.

And therein, also,
began his skepticism
of prayer,
his faith unraveling
like a runaway
ball of yarn.

-Jen Wieber

Chapter 82:

The Painter

(Trigger Warning: Suicide)

Last summer, when the magnolia trees were in full bloom, he set out a ladder and grabbed a brush and, one shingle at a time, painted the drab brown house a promising sage green.

It took him over two months, meticulous strokes, the ladder rotating around the house in two feet sections, so slowly one would need to blink to make sure they were seeing clearly.

"Saves money!" He said, with that infectious laugh of his, and he didn't care that it would take him all summer.

He'd take frequent breaks so that he could spend time with his daughters. The way they looked at him, he was their moon. He could make them laugh.

He'd take them to swim practice and then come right back to paint some more and finally, at the end of the summer, it was finished.

He shot a bullet through his brain the following winter on a cold January morning. Debt and guilt and despair spattered over the wall in bright scarlet hues. Alone in the house.

The painted sage house.

I walked by the other day after the moving trucks were long gone and noticed the magnolia tree, stark and naked. It was hugging the corner near the kitchen window just like always but it looked different, odd. Through the limbs I could see a ragged brown rectangle. I walked closer to inspect. To tremble. The drab brown rectangle is a spot missed by the meticulous painter. The leaves then had been so robust, so hopeful that the painter hadn't seen the spot he'd missed.

But that was then—when the magnolia tree was in full, fucking bloom. Now it sits undressed in the unforgiving winter. The brown rectangle taunts as the wind bites through my thin layer.

That spring, after a for-sale sign was pounded into the thawing ground, an idyllic family drives up to look at the house, the painted sage house, and I hear the tweed jacket lady telling her husband that sage is a drab color and that she must have white. I imagined her pinched face, inches from the scarlet splatters of grief and loneliness but they must have been painted over with a pristine cover because she came out the door with a look of triumph on her face, shaking hands with the agent and then driving away. I wanted to take a knife and cut out her calloused expectation. I wanted to scream at her. Tell her that sage is the color he wanted. I wanted to tell her how long it took him. I wanted to tell her to leave it sage.

With a choked sob I imagine the painter in the cold, hard ground, thinking he had finished painting the sage green house.

Who will drive the car to swim practice?

Who will make them laugh.

-Jen Wieber

Chapter 83:

Idaho

You know it's been a good vacation
when you come home with a pair of steer horns.

That, and the way the golden sunlight
has attached itself to your shoulders,
making the very art of breathing easier.

And the way we continue
to fall asleep each night,
breath matching breath,
our fingers entwined.

-Jen Wieber

About Jen Wieber

Jen (She/Her/Hers) is a writer from Boise, ID. The best souvenirs are those we experience with our entire beings and then collect in our minds. Poetry is a way for her to collect the souvenirs she experiences each day. You can find her at jenwieber.com

Jessica Zarrillo

Chapter 84:

Struck

like midnight:
a countdown to 12 and that fucking kiss and the look you gave me as
we broke away, only one of us knowing what was to live next on your
tongue. *like magic:* your bewitched eyes dilating and reflecting the
TV screen brighter than all 2,688 waterford crystals; my first, middle,
and last name pouring out from your lips and sparkling like
champagne. *like a spell:* each word in "will you be my girlfriend?"
immortalized in my saturated brain watching all your walls crumble.
like a bargain: "okay. you get to keep my heart now", bleary-happy
and burying your silly blonde hair into my nape. *like a moment*: never
to be forgotten.

like lightning:
a weblike tattoo sprawling across my backbone at record speed,
invisible ink trailing the trace of every individual goosebump you
imprint. *like electricity*: 1,000 (giga)volts zapping your chest in
attempt to induce a normal heartbeat (with an added 50% chance to
either paralyze or pulverize). *like awe:* wanting so hard I witness it in
physical sparks of blue-white static bunny-hopping across your faux-
fur comforter in the dark. *like moon:* untrammeled tippy-taps
escaping from my toes and imagined superpowers leaking from
fingertips; *like stars:* too fascinated to even attempt to pull away from
this magnetism.

like a match:
igniting a wildfire spreading from my coast to yours. *like while the
iron is hot:* 'no smoking' signs and blustery winds stopping no one,
just cupped hands and laced fingers shielding our flame. *like force:* an
unstoppable might on piggyback made from equal parts Sour Patch
Kids and sriracha mayo. *like dumb:* speechless and nestled into the
warmth of our flame, watching the stars rearrange themselves in the
night sky for us. *like luck:* the very same sobriquet uniting us from
'hatches' to 'despatches'; a very special joke crafted just for us, and
an introduction that never gets less funny. *like gold*: not a damn thing

ever again in this lifetime coming close to this fire in my belly when we kiss.

-Jessica Zarrillo

Chapter 85:

July Recalls a Wedding That Never Happened on a Mountain That Never Existed

He thinks that he can accustom himself to suffering. It pains me that he's half right, but he's only being half-serious. Being the lone point of his fixation was akin to navigating interstellar space, and we'd escape any time gravity got too heavy to hold. He often used faulty science to convince me that time was standing still.

Floating aimlessly through the galaxy relieves him of this chore of ever planting seeds. Love can never blossom deprived of oxygen and he's far too hyper-focused on the big picture to stop and smell the roses, nevermind getting to the root of his issues. Trauma bonding through difficult years helps to ensure I grow fond of each delicate one.

"You aren't a bad son" is something I say aloud and it festers, becoming a sentiment I latch onto perennially and in reiteration, freckled years spent pounding this point into the ground. You just had a sick dad with the kind of sickness that seeps into their sons. The excuses almost weave themselves as we slip between garnet moons, and you learn to say "I love you" looking for echoes. You always find them.

One day ten years into our friendship you say, "Most of the time, I'm the source of my own pain," a strange, candid billow of smoke exhaled between entire lungfuls of hot air. Only then does it hit me that isn't how it should be.

The eternities I've plucked loving him are long wilted, and he's the shadow of the man he could've been. When I still let myself love him, the ugliest warmth is born in the pit of my belly like a nightmare made of cinnamon whiskey, gasoline, and open flames. I inhale his smoke as my own sustenance.

I too am sick, and drunk on every single part of him, and he scorches my throat the whole way down.

-Jessica Zarrillo

Chapter 86:

Splinter Theory

It's taken me eons to finish your pages, eternity lost to haggard breaths
in prolonged spaces and desperate attempts to make rhythm out of
Nothing. All those years *had to* mean something, so I refuge the tiniest
reminders of him on my shelves like sick background decor and
harbor scraps of him in soggy boxes in the closet. In between every
comma, I identify new holes in our story.

Certain details remain frozen in the landscape of my brain, chiseled
out from toxic hope and a relationship forged on codependency.
Does my grief have a heart? I ask in a telltale screaming fit I force
upon the wall. Knowing I'll never duck on my own, God coaches me
to stop, drop, and roll with the punches.

You asked what we could be — like we hadn't long broken; like you
hadn't been the fabric of my Everything, or my biggest reason not to
un-alive; like for a second, you were carving out your own space
for tough answers. It's a shame you used your hands; you didn't dig
deep enough and now your palms are plagued with splinters.

Tell me which is worse: Lukewarm love, empty attraction, or having
to choose between the two at every intersection? I don't dream right
anymore now that I know exactly what a closet space is worth in
Astoria.

My therapist tried to remind me: *To be someone's rock is also to be their*
whetstone. All those years, I'd had the never-ending nerve to use him
for sharpening my tongue. And still, I found myself surprised at just
how cutting he'd become.

Like I hadn't been the splinter.

-Jessica Zarrillo

About Jessica Zarrillo

Jessica Zarrillo (She/Her) is a writer from Long Island. If she can't be favored by the stars, she will favor the shit out of her friends across the globe. You can find her at jesszarr.com

⭕ SourNothings

Anonymous

Chapter 87:

(untitled)

I find myself drifting into the replays of the moments when our faces were pressed together.

My memory effortlessly recalls burying my face deep into the crevasse of your beard and neck.

Remember when I delicately followed your chin line up with my tongue until my mouth completely engulfed your ear?

Soft pecks of my lips across your cheek until our lips meet together strongly and our entire bodies arch.

I have to ground myself by cradling your face with my hands.

You abruptly change the tempo and shower me with adoration by giving me many quick pecks of your squishy lips all over the front of my face.

Our tongues meet again to intertwine in play.

I softly pull away with your lower lip between my teeth, nibbling as I stare deeply into your green eyes.

Our energetic exchange instinctually ebbs and flows.

I enjoy turning you on and you encourage me to fill your fantasy by being one of the many facets of myself, a dominating woman.

And with relief my body thanks you when you retake the lead, allowing my mind to relax and for once relinquish all strength to expose where I am soft.

At this moment, I trust you. Together, we are innately both the leader and the follower.

You press our lips together firmly as you forcefully rub your hands all over my body.

Caressing my breasts and pulling my hair, I become increasingly wet for you.

Your hands search for the natural hand holds of my body to pull me closer and position me perfectly so we can both imagine you inside of me.

Our imaginations are powerful as we start to believe what we are experiencing in our minds.

We open our mouths to gasp for air, backing away slightly leaving only a single point of contact between our lips as we breathe in and out each other's breaths.

We hold each other's gaze and our bodies tightly, neither of us dare part in fear that ceasing the existence of this moment will mortally cease the existence of us.

Without too much thought, we created meaning to life's existentialism with our desire to elongate these moments together where we lose sight of our individual edges and merge into one entity. I torture myself by living in these memory loops because my brain cannot discern the emotions elicited by the replay from the actual event.

Chapter 88:

Priorities

You needed love,
I needed you.

You needed warmth caressing your heart,
you needed softness overwhelming you.

You needed two parts oxygen,
I needed fire.

I needed you
gasping, groveling and lying on the exhale as my lungs collapse;
I needed all of you
consuming me, your breath on my neck.
I needed your touch;
the tip of your tongue
at the edge of my bones,
the ends of your fingers
holding me down
as I arch my back
into the secret world
you've breathed into my soul.
Hot heart, hot sigh.

You needed love,
I needed you,
I needed you falling apart into me.
It was never going to work
no matter the wreckage
nor the love that split the world.

You needed love,
I needed you.

Chapter 89:

Without Words

Everything around us slowed down.
The sea became still.
The chaos paused.
The town silenced.
Time stopped.

I wondered how I could know a man so well,
Without needing the use of words.
As I looked into the vastness of his eyes,
The universe held my hand while yelling my name.
I found my biggest fan.

I slipped underneath him and spread my legs.
Connecting each other by placing my right hand on his heart and left
upon mine,
I gave myself fully to him.
I am yours, I said with my eyes.

This moment wasn't about me,
It was for him.
I was contributing to creating space for his full expression.
I gave him full control of his pleasure without any need to
reciprocate.

As he penetrated me, we ferociously held each other's steady stare.
Tears erupted and started shedding down his cheeks.
Dripping off his chin onto my hand and flowing down my arm.
Eventually, falling off my elbow and pooling on my belly.

I held open the space that he didn't know he needed.
He allowed himself to feel.
I was strong, yet soft, as he pressed into me.
He processed his emotions through sex and pleasure.
I assured him that the space was safe with my gaze,
As he unexpectedly released lifetimes of sorrow.

At that moment, I understood love.
True love.
The real kind.
The kind that doesn't need words to exist.

Chapter 90:

<u>Bile</u>

self-importance in the name of grace
weighs so heavily on your eyelids that
you can never see the Thursday
in September from the year that
never ended when your beloved
tumbled with me crotch-first into
a cemetery somewhere along the
side of a road.
and my stomach turns
with his bile
in the browning grass.

Chapter 91:

Questions I would ask (if the potential answers didn't terrify me.)

1 How do you quiet a mind?
2 What is stillness if I'm choking?
3 Does fear get full (after devouring us)?
4 Why is it darkest on a Sunday night?
5 Is forever too long to love you?
6 Why do I look in the mirror and see a villain?
7 Why does this shrapnel taste a lot like missing you?
8 Can you keep a promise?
9 What if you decide you don't want this?
10 ~~What if you don't stay?~~   How do I survive?

Chapter 92:

(Untitled)

Call it electric. See the sparks.
Shout fire in a crowded room.

It is the sweltering heat building in a belly.

A clench in the toes, an arrhythmia between two legs. A willow tree
spine.

A longing to feel flannel against skin.
A longing for skin against skin.
For floor and flannel to meet.

For more. More. *Always more.*
Insatiable, incorrigible —
inward, inward, inward.

The sky shifts. The world tilts.
And I linger, linger, linger.

Chapter 93:

(Untitled)

He and I live in a world of what if's.
Where he longs to know the length of my throat, and I ache to come
to the sound of his breathing. Where I feel electricity miles away,
picturing mountains, my breasts heaving. Imagining wind between
trees, pushing his pulse into me.

Oh, what if he could be mine? What if I could be his? We exist in a
realm so perfect not even the gods could throttle my reach for him.
There are no interruptions here. Only sandalwood and pine and forest
friction. Volcanic tension.

Where we are together, where I leave what is safe, what is settled,
what is familiar. Where I can't deny him any longer. Where it's stolen
shirts, and family barbecues, and wild, wild love. Such absurd
sweetness and reverie basking in charcoal smoke and backyard
hammocks.

Carnal eyes and barbaric fantasies. Where survival means only air,
while all else bottoms out.

Chapter 94:

smell (double-dipping)

We stole exactly one night away in
July 2019. I'll never forget your new
smell, or the musk of the hotel room
fifteen miles from your apartment,
half naked and too nervous about
your girlfriend to fall asleep. There's
an awful look on your face as you

tell me to clean yourself up, then
come cuddle ...you had pushed for
this in the first place, but you push
me away. "I've always had a problem
with double-dipping," you admit to me
unprompted. "I've cheated on every
girlfriend I've ever had." I realize that
I really am your best friend.

I took a pill the morning after.

As far as I know, in this lifetime,
I never smell you again.

Chapter 95:

(untitled)

I do my best writing keeping company with the dead.
I have always known I was a witch.
Visions and past life memories flooded my thoughts,
Before I knew what visions and past life memories were.
And I knew my soul was damned.
Every week a reminder
I was wretched.
I packed my visions into tiny boxes inside my mind.
Threw myself into the holy waters.

I decided I would preach the gospel,
I knew I was meant to be seen
Be known.
I would be a shining light for god.
Except gospel preaching was not for people like me,
Without a male organ hanging between my legs.

I was fired for being gay.
Women and queers do not belong in the pulpit.
But that would not stop me from trying.
To be a holy temple
Allowing the light of the most high to shine through me.
If I could not preach I would sing
And sing
And sing.
Until my voice was hoarse
From singing my own damnation.

I walked away from the church
From a religion that offered me no salvation
Unless I cut out the very essence of my soul
And burned it on the Do This In Remembrance of Me altar.

I returned to my roots.
Let them stretch long and deep
Into the stabilizing ground of my ancestors
Of my ancient selves
Of love
Loyalty
Peace.

Chapter 96:

teethmarks

maybe i just like to love in little
segments, presenting digestible,
bite-sized pieces of my heart for
my master to chew on. (or maybe
i'm just getting ready to choke.)
maybe we inherit the way we love
from our parents. or perhaps our
behavior is woven into the spirals
of our dna. you can identify me
either way by my dental records.

Chapter 97:

(untitled)

I'm having dinner with my partner
And all I can think about is fucking the waitress.
So I look into her eyes a little too long,
Catch the gleam there,
Give her a sly smile.
And now the waitress knows that all I can think about is fucking the
waitress.
We exchange glances at every opportunity.
I ask for the restroom and she follows. Slips inside the single stall.
We are feral,
aggressive,
No romance.
Nothing tender.
Donna Summer plays through the speakers.
"Bad girl, sad girl, you're such a naughty bad girl."
I cover her mouth with mine as she comes.
We walk out as if nothing has occurred.

"You feeling ok? You look flushed."
I assure my partner I am fine.
Finish dinner.
Enjoy the complimentary dessert.
It is my turn to pay and they grab their card.
A display.
A stand.
A claim.